Contents

KU-024-900

Twisted Tales

GHOST STORIES

MICHAEL COX

Illustrated by Michael Tickner

■SCHOLASTIC

Scholastic Children's Books,
Commonwealth House, 1-19 New Oxford Street, London WC1A 1NU, UK

A division of Scholastic Ltd
London ~ New York ~ Toronto ~ Sydney ~ Auckland
Mexico City ~ New Delhi ~ Hong Kong

First published in the UK under the series title *Top Ten* by Scholastic Ltd, 2001
This edition published 2004

Text copyright © Michael Cox, 2001
Illustrations copyright © Michael Tickner, 2001

ISBN 0 439 96359 1

Typeset by Falcon Oast Graphic Art, East Hoathly, East Sussex.
Printed and bound by Nørhaven Paperback A/S, Denmark

2 4 6 8 10 9 7 5 3 1

The right of Michael Cox and Michael Tickner to be identified as the author and
illustrator of this work respectively has been asserted by them in accordance with the
Copyright, Designs and Patents Act, 1988.

Introduction

Have you ever been in a room and thought that you were all on your own then suddenly got the horrible feeling that there was another "presence" there with you? Or maybe you've been walking your pet dog (or gerbil) through some lonely woods when it's suddenly "frozen" in its tracks, growling ferociously, with the hairs on its back standing on end as it seems to "see" something that *you* can't!

Well, if you have had this sort of experience some people would tell you that you may have encountered some sort of ghost, or the wandering "spirit" of someone who's died, then returned from the "other side". Ooer!

However, lots of *other* people would tell you you're a hysterical twit who ought to have better things to do with your time (such as taking your dog to see an optician more frequently!).

People have probably been arguing and puzzling over whether ghosts do or don't exist ever since that forgettable foggy October morning when an over-imaginative Ancient Briton mistook a man carrying a very large turnip for the ghost of a Saxon warrior he'd decapitated a few weeks earlier. Over the years all sorts of experts and investigators have carried out masses of enquiries and scientific tests to try and discover the truth about spooks. But they're *still* none the wiser! There seems to be no completely reliable way of proving or disproving the existence of ghosts. And *that's* what makes reading and telling ghost stories such fun! Because all the time you're thinking...

Especially when the pages of your book begin turning all on their own...

SORRY, I CAN'T WAIT TO FIND OUT WHAT HAPPENS NEXT. TERRIFYING, ISN'T IT?

And it's also why the writers of great ghost stories like the ones in this book have such fun dreaming them up in order to scare themselves and their readers completely shirtless. Some of the following tales of spooks 'n' spectres are funny, some are sad and quite a few are really, really frightening.

OK! You've no excuse for delaying any longer ... now it's time for *you* to cross over to the "other side" (of the page, that is!). There's a seance taking place there right now – so go and join it. But before you do, a note of warning. Whatever you do, *do not* read this book in a darkened room ... you'll never be able to make out the words.

How It Happened

The story that first floats wispily into view is by Sir Arthur Conan Doyle (1859–1930), the creator of ace detective, Sherlock Holmes. After his crime and mystery tales had made him rich and famous, Sir Arthur got really interested in another sort of mystery. The puzzle of what happens to people after they're dead and whether it's possible to communicate with them.

He became a big believer in spiritualism (the idea that the living can contact the dead) and attempted to get in touch with his dead chums through a spiritualist go-between known as a medium. It's said that confidence tricksters and dodgy mediums fooled him into believing they'd successfully made his old pals materialize by showing him photographs of himself with their "ghosts". But what they'd actually done was to cut the faces from photographs of his friends, stick them on negatives of pictures of Sir Arthur, then print them to give him the impression he was being rejoined by his departed buddies. Amazing that the inventor of the sharpest sleuth in crime fiction didn't "detect" that tacky scam, isn't it? Despite people pointing out that he'd been tricked, Sir Arthur continued to believe in ghosts and the power of mediums to contact the dead. No doubt that's what led to him dreaming up this great little story. "How It Happened" was written in 1913 but this version's been brought up to date a bit.

The ghost writer

As the tearful fans waited with bated breath the medium picked up her pen, paused for a moment, then began to write.

At first the words came slowly but after a few moments the pen began to move across the paper confidently and swiftly. Soon she was writing with the utmost urgency, as if she just had to get the words down, no matter what!

It was as if her hand was directed by a force so strong that her fingers were entirely powerless to resist it. In other words, a force ... from beyond the grave! This is what it wrote:

I can remember tons of stuff about that night really well! Me and the band had just finished a sell-out tour of America and had flown into Heathrow at around 5 p.m., UK time. The tour was a <u>WOW!</u> Packed stadiums every night with me and the Squiffheads giving it everything we'd got and our American fans going nuts for more. It did wonders for our CD sales and Carmen Crocodile, my press agent, had E-mailed me on Concorde to say that "Raw Pudding" by Nick Ramsbottom and the Squiffheads had gone straight into the number one spot in the US charts. Way to go, guy! But crikey, was I bushed!

After we'd come through customs there was the usual mob of adoring fans yelling and waving so I signed a few autographs and kissed a few crazy chicks' cheeks which got them sobbing and fainting as usual. And that made me think, "Talk about a dream come true! Eight chart-busting singles, my own yacht in the mediterranean and a mansion in Surrey! All at the tender age of twenty-five!"

After I'd had a quick laugh and a joke with the boys from Melody Express and Prime Slime I came out of Terminal 2... and there it was! My pride and joy. My new toy, just waiting for me...

its tail fins glinting in the late-afternoon sun, top down, its engine purring like a panther on the prowl as old Jagger playfully buzzed the accelerator. And it looked better than I'd ever imagined it would! My very own 1953 pink Cadillac El Dorado convertible!

The guy who bought all my cars for me had found it just before we flew to the States. So I hadn't actually had a chance to see it until now... never mind drive it!

JAGGER

But it had been neglected by its previous owner and needed to go into Mad About Caddies for a refit and a major overhaul, so that wasn't really a problem.

As Jagger slid over to the passenger seat, I vaulted in and playfully grabbed his peaked chauffeur's cap from his bald head and set it on top of my own mass of luxuriant curls, getting a big laugh from the fans and the press. Then, with a screech of tyres, we left the airport. I reckoned that if the traffic on the M25 wasn't too bad we should make my Surrey mansion by sundown. Then for some serious chilling out!

Well the M25 was bad. But what did I care! I was a megastar, I had my new wheels, the sun was shining, the top was down and Chuck Berry was blasting out on my newly fitted CD player! I sure felt sorry for those pathetic commuter types casting their envious glances at me as they crawled drearily home from their sad little office jobs in the city!

So everything was GREAT... until we came to the top of Claystall Hill, which leads down to the gates of Squiffy Acres, my place in the country. It's one of the worst hills in England, about a mile and a half long, with a gradient that's as steep as 35% in places... and two killer bends too! It's the sort of hill that would have made

SQUIFFY ACRES

the stuff fall out of the Caddie's glove
compartment had we been climbing it!
But we weren't. We were going down!
We'd just topped the brow and started
the long descent when the
trouble began. I touched the
brakes to slow us just a tad
and nothing happened. That's
right... zilch ... zero... nothing!
"Hey, Jagger!" I said. "Are you
sure those guys finished that refit
properly?"

"Well, sir," he replied a bit sheepishly, as
we began to gather speed. "They did have
rather short notice. You said you wanted it
ready today, come what may! When I
picked it up they did say they could have
done with another couple of days! To
double-check the safety devices! This
car is nearly 50 years old, sir."

As Jagger was giving me this unwelcome
news I was pumping the brake
pedal for all I was worth
and the Caddie was picking
up speed by the second. Luckily
there was no other traffic on the hill
so at least we had a clear run ahead
of us. My mansion's in a pretty remote
spot. When we were up to 60. m.p.h.
Jagger said, "Might I suggest that sir
tries the handbrake as the others

all seem to have failed."

"Great idea, man!" I yelled and seized the brake lever and hauled on it with all my strength. Which is probably why it came away in my hand!

"Oh cripes!" I screamed, slinging the brake lever over my shoulder. "Any more bright ideas, Jags?"

"Might I suggest that sir bangs the gears into reverse?" Jagger yelled back. Which I did immediately, only to hear the sickening sound of teeth being stripped from cogs as the gearbox disintegrated. The first bend was coming up and I was wishing I hadn't unfastened my seat-belt ten minutes earlier (a bad habit of mine but something I always did when I was almost home and feeling cool!). I gripped the wheel and with all my might I steered her into a camber like I was a Formula One racing ace. And we made the first bend!

"Sorted!" I yelled. "One down... one to go, Jags!"

"Well done, sir," said Jagger. "But I think the next one's going to be much, much harder." He was right too. The next bend, which was about a mile ahead was much sharper. And just around it were the big gates of my house.

So it was going to be very, very tricky. But! But! If I could just get the Caddie through them in one piece, we'd be fine and dandy. The big tree-lined drive to the house was uphill and that would bring us to a stop... no problem!

During that final mile Jagger was brilliant! Ice cool and completely sharp! At one point I was thinking of running the Caddie up the bank at the side of the lane and stopping it that way but the cunning old fox seemed to read my mind in an instant.

"I shouldn't do that if I were you, sir," he said. "You'll flip her over at this speed!" Then he reached over, switched off the ignition, put his hands on the wheel and said, "Look here, sir. If you care to chance it and jump out now, I'll keep her steady while you do. We're never going to make that last bend, sir. Never!"

I mean, talk about loyalty. Wadda hero! "No thanks, Jags man!" I said. "I'm seeing this baby through! But you're welcome to bail out if you like."

"No thank you, sir," he replied, calm as a kumquat. "I think I'll stick with you, if you don't mind."

"OK, man!" I yelled. "Get the remote control

ready to open the big gates. And the moment we get close enough... zap 'em!"

We went into that last bend with one wheel up the bank. I was sure we'd flip over. But we didn't. We made that second corner brilliantly.

"Yahoo! Way to go, Jagger baby! Zap that remote!" I yelled, as we shot out of the lane and straight towards the big gates.

Well, I don't know what it was, but in my excitement and relief I must have taken my hand off the wheel and punched the air or something (an on-stage habit of mine). As I did I knocked the remote straight of Jagger's hand and sent it flying. So the gates stayed closed! And we hit them like a rocket going nowhere! Next thing I knew I was flying through the air, and then... and then....!

When I came to I was amongst the bushes under the big oak trees at the side of the drive. There was another guy standing next to me. At first I thought it was Jagger, but when I looked at him again I saw it was Baz Gallagher from my old band, Spiral Codpiece.

"Good old Baz!" I thought. "One of the best! Always great for a laugh! I'll never forget the night me and him rode that hostess trolley into the pool at the Honshu Hilton! And neither will the hostess! Hahaha!"

To be honest with you, I was quite surprised to see Baz standing there. But then again I was feeling a bit like a bloke in a dream, all shook up and dizzy and that. So I thought no more of it!

"By heck... wadda wreck! I've gone and pranged my beautiful, beautiful Caddie!" I said to Baz.

Baz nodded his head and even though it was nearly dark, I could see that he was smiling. That unmistakeable and reassuring old Baz smile that I'd seen him smile a thousand times before!

"Good old Baz!" I thought. "One of the best!"

I couldn't move a muscle. Even if I'd wanted to! But to be quite honest, I didn't want to. I was quite happy to be there in the bushes with Baz. Even though I couldn't actually move, my senses felt as right as rain! I could see my wrecked Caddie up against the gates. It looked like it had hit them head on, then flipped back on itself. Talk about "mashed up"! Torch beams were playing over the mangled metal and there was a whole gang of people gathered around it and all talking sort of quiet like. Funny thing is they were so busy with the wreck they didn't even seem to notice me.

"The weight's on him!" I heard one of them say. "Lift it as carefully as you can."

"It's only my leg," said another voice which I recognized straight away! It was Jagger. "Great!" I thought. "He's made it too!"

A moment later I heard him say, "Where's Mr Ramsbottom? Is he OK?"

"Hey you guys!" I yelled. "I'm over here! In the cotton pickin' bushes. Under the big oak trees! Look! Here! Are you lot blind... or what!"

But amazingly enough they all just ignored me and carried on milling around the wreck and whatnot! And then I noticed that they'd all gathered around something that lay on the drive about twenty metres in front of the Caddie. As I tried to make out what it was they were all looking at I felt Baz's hand on my shoulder. His touch was sort of reassuring and soothing and really gentle! Suddenly I felt amazingly happy and lighthearted. Even though I had just pranged my pride and joy and half-killed my chauffeur!

"No pain, of course?" said Baz.

"No! None at all, mate. Sound as a pound!" I replied.

"There never is," said Baz.

At that moment a big sort of shudder of amazement and disbelief and shock blasted right through me as something suddenly clicked.

"Baz? Baz! Good old Baz Gallagher! Standing here next to me?" I thought. "But didn't Baz get electrocuted when his electric guitar short-circuited on-stage at Wembley Stadium! He died just moments later! The roadie that set up the equipment was put on a manslaughter charge!

"Baz!" I yelled, but I could hardly get the words out because they were sticking in my throat and choking me! "But Baz?!" I cried. "You're ... you're ... dead!"

"And so are you," said Baz.

Things you've always wanted to know about ghosts

So, what are ghosts all about? And is that really what it would be like to be a ghost? No one knows for sure but here are the answers to some ghostly FAQs (Frequently Asked Questions).

What actually is a ghost?
A ghost is thought to be the life spirit or "soul" of a human or an animal. Some people believe that ghosts only exist in the minds of the people who claim to have seen them. The senses are strange things and often play sneaky tricks on their human owners, especially if those owners are tired, nervous, upset, really desperate to believe in something, or just desperately dim.

Even though the world is bursting at the seams with computers, worldwide web-sites and databases the size of Alaska, very little is known about the mysterious human mind and the way it works. Even less (or to be honest, absolutely zilch!) is known about what happens to people after they finally cash in their carpet slippers and float off to the mystic megastore in the sky. It's all very weird, mysterious and frustrating – but that's exactly what makes the subject of ghosts so interesting and exciting, isn't it?

YES, MAYBE FOR YOU MATE! BUT YOU'VE NOT GOT TO SPEND ALL ETERNITY WANDERING AROUND DAMP CASTLES, RATTLING CHAINS AND GROANING LIKE A BISHOP WITH A BELLY-ACHE!

What is the first ever recorded sighting of a ghost?

One of the first descriptions of a ghost sighting was written down about 2,000 years ago by a Roman writer called Pliny the Younger. This "rattling" good yarn was about a house in the Greek city of Athens that no one would stay at because it was supposed to be haunted. A Greek philosopher called Athenodorus rented the house and soon came face to face with an apparition so awful that it was said to have caused a previous tenant to die of fright! One evening Athenodorus was having a quiet philosophize when he heard the sound of a chain being pulled. He rushed off to investigate and came face to face with an old man with long, shaggy white hair and an even longer, even shaggier white beard, who was all wrapped in chains. The old chap clanked and rattled his way out to the

WHO PULLED YOUR CHAIN?!

garden, pointed to a spot in the earth, then disappeared. This set off a chain reaction, and the next day Athenodorus and the local bigwig unearthed a skellybob at the very place the apparition had pointed to! It was trussed up in rusty chains. Athenodorus and the bigwig immediately spotted the link (sorry, *links*) between the skelly and the apparition. They quickly reburied "Boney Maroney" at a local graveyard and the haunting stopped from that day on. Phew!

Important note: Some people think this is just a "shaggy ghost story" that Pliny dreamed up to entertain his pals.

Why doesn't everyone have a ghost?

Ghosts are usually associated with sudden or violent death. Some people believe that the shock of a really unexpected send-off makes the soul leave the body too quickly.

In other words, it gets booted into touch before it's actually ready to be beamed up to wherever souls go when they're no longer trapped inside the disgusting lump of guts, gristle and gunge that pretentious people like to call their "body". Perhaps it's like getting a power cut just when you're in the middle of watching a really exciting telly programme then being left all "up in the air", wondering what was going to happen next and not quite ready for total chill-out status?

What is a medium?
A medium is a person who claims to have extreme sensitivity which enables them to contact the spirits of the dead. Mediums are said to be "telepathic". This doesn't mean they spend the whole day slumped in front of the idiot box because they can't be bothered to switch it off. It means they have special powers, like being able to tell what other people are thinking, and being able to project their own thoughts to other people without actually saying them or writing them down ... oooer! And with powers like that, who needs TV! Finally, just to make matters entirely clear, it is important to realize that some mediums are actually quite large, whilst others are really, really small.

What is a seance?
A seance is a meeting organized by people who are trying to contact the spirits of the dead. They usually do

this through a medium. The medium acts as a sort of living internet provider who helps people to get through to the web-sites of the dead ... sort of. Seances are usually held in darkened rooms. It is thought that they work best if no more than eight people are present (not counting ghosts, of course).

The seancers sit around a table with their hands flat on top of it and their fingers touching, or interlocked if they're feeling really friendly. Sometimes they play music or chat as they wait for the ghost to turn up. The whole idea is to create a pleasant and soothing atmosphere that will encourage the spirits of the dead to pop in for a chat. Old castles, country houses and churches are reckoned to be the best places to hold seances. They hardly ever take place at crowded beaches, rowdy discotheques or football stadiums on Cup Final day. The seancers wait patiently for something to happen and, if they're lucky, they will eventually hear knocking sounds, see a strange light, or feel a blast of cold air – or maybe all three if the ghost is in the mood for showing off. This tells them that the spirit has finally arrived ... or that Uncle Fred's turned up late for the seance again!

The seancers now begin to ask the ghostly presence questions through the medium of the medium.

Sometimes the medium communicates the ghost's answers through "automatic writing" in which the ghost controls their pen and makes them scribble down whatever it wants to say. Yes, just like in Sir Arthur's story! At other times the medium uses a thing called a ouija board to get the replies from the ghost. So, would you like to ask another question?

Yes please. What is a ouija board?
What a brilliant question! The ouija board was invented in the USA in 1892, by Elija Bond. It's a bit like scrabble for ghosts. Its name comes from "oui" (the French word for "yes") and "ja" (the German word for "yes") so it's actually called the "yesyes" board.

There are letters and numbers and words all over it. The medium places a little three-legged platform with a pointer on the board, then begins to ask the ghosts questions on behalf of the people at the seance.

The ghost doesn't actually speak its reply, but it uses its supernatural powers to make the pointer platform mysteriously move to the answer on the board.

Important point! The fact that the medium has their finger on the little platform has nothing to do with the fact that it actually moves to the answer. The ghost is making the medium move it for them ... honest!

The people at the seance often ask after the health of the ghost (e.g. "Apart from being dead, are you OK?") and the ghost generally gives them the answers they want to hear (e.g. "Yes, not bad at all thanks, considering the circumstances!"). This has nothing to do with the fact that the people with the questions are paying the medium money for the seance and the medium wants them to leave in a happy and satisfied mood so they will book them for another seance and give them some more money. Honest!

Touching fact: Ouija boards became really popular just after World War One when they were used by lots of heartbroken people who were desperate to get in touch with the hundreds of thousands of loved ones who'd been killed in that big wasteful botch up.

What is "ectoplasm" when it's at home?

Ectoplasm is the disgusting gungey stuff that sometimes comes squirting out of the bodies of mediums when they get overexcited. If you look at photographs of old-time mediums doing their stuff you can often see great dollops of it pouring out of their noses – just like giant, white "bogey spaghetti" ... no kidding! It also comes out of their ears and mouths and other places far too personal to mention. One famous medium called Marthe Beraud produced dancing ectoplasm that writhed about like octopus tentacles whenever anyone tried to touch it. (There's always someone who has to go one better, isn't there?)

Sometimes ectoplasm transforms itself into the shape of extra arms and legs which are called pseudopods. At other times it moulds itself into the shape of the faces or bodies of people who have died. All of this is extremely frightening / exciting / fascinating (delete as applicable) for anybody daft enough not to realize that ectoplasm is actually just a load of dribble / egg whites / soap / cotton wool / paper / cloth ... or whatever else the medium has had tucked up their sleeve / nose / armpit / earhole!

What is "an out of body experience"?
During an out of body experience, or OOBE, as they're known to fans, people get the feeling that they are actually leaving their own bodies and floating in space, possibly in much the same way that a soul or "spirit" is

thought to "float" out of a body when it dies. This usually occurs if the person has a really close brush with death. Perhaps during a routine head-transplant operation or blindfold cliff-edge stroll that goes unexpectedly wrong!

People who have had OOBEs but have survived often describe the feeling of being drawn towards a bright light and of "hovering" in space and looking down at their own body.

They also say they had the feeling they could choose between dying and living. And guess which option they went for!

How long do ghosts live for?

What do you mean "live"? They're dead ... aren't they? So they can go on for ever if they like! Having said that, some ghosts *don't* exist for ever. They just fade away. In the early eighteenth century a woman ghost dressed in a bright red dress and shoes was regularly seen haunting an old house. She wasn't spotted again until about 70 years later, but by now her crimson frock had faded to pink. By the time the mid-nineteenth century arrived the ghost woman's dress had become white and her hair had turned completely grey. By the early twentieth century you couldn't even *see* the old dear any more! All you could hear was the rustle of her dress and her ghostly footsteps (and the sound of her voice going on about how *rude* young ghosts were and how it

hadn't been like that in her day and how she wouldn't be seen *dead* in one of those newfangled mini-skirts!). In 1971 you couldn't even *hear* her, she was just a ghostly presence felt by the workmen who'd finally been brought in to demolish the haunted house!

Are ghosts dangerous?

Not necessarily, although the shock of seeing a ghost has sometimes caused people to have a heart attack ... and perhaps become a ghost themselves. If you're worried about coming to harm at the hands of a ghost (quite literally), you should definitely avoid the stretch of road between Twobridges and Postbridge on Dartmoor in Devon, England. It's said that an evil presence lurks there in the shape of a pair of huge hairy mitts! In 1921 a man was tootling along on his motorbike with a couple of children in the sidecar when he veered off the road for no apparent reason. He yelled a warning to the kids who jumped clear and survived, but he was killed. The children later described seeing two enormous hairy hands gripping the handlebars of the wrecked motorbike just moments after the crash!

Some months later another motorcyclist described how two giant hairy mitts had closed over his own hands and forced him off the road. Other people claim to have had similar experiences at the hands of the, er ... hairy hands!

However, on the other hand(s), some ghosts are actually thought to be kind and helpful. One ghost grabbed hold of a factory worker in Detroit in America and saved his life by pulling him out of the way of some falling machinery. It was said to be the ghost of a man who'd died in a similar accident 20 years previously.

So listen! If you do meet a ghost, don't immediately run off screaming! It might be there to give you a hand – which is fine, as long as it's not a pair of huge hairy ones!

The Turn of the Screw

The Turn of the Screw (1898) is by American writer Henry James (1843–1916), and it's about a woman who goes to teach and look after two orphan children at a country estate in Essex. She hasn't been there long when two ghostly presences arrive and give her all sorts of terrible frights and problems, especially as they seem to be after the nippers! When the problems start she doesn't know which way to turn and gets herself into a right old tizz! Henry James set the story in his own Victorian times, but in this version, it's been brought up to date. So the worried woman can pick up the phone and dial one of those late night radio "chat-ins"...

18th May

Al Mighty: Hi, all you lonely ones. The one and only Al Mighty here again, providing sad and troubled folk *everywhere* with a shoulder to cry on. And playing you some *smooooth* and *grooooovy* sounds. *Yhair!* First call's from a Miss Terry. She wants a bit of advice about a job.

Miss Terry: Yes, er ... hello. I've been offered a job as private teacher to two little orphaned children. The money's very good and I'll be living in their big posh house in the countryside with them and all their servants and ponies and whatnot.

Al: So what's your problem then, m'dear?

Miss T: Well, the gentleman what's offered me the job is the children's rich uncle and he's gone off to live in London now. He says if I take the job I must never *ever* contact him again. Not never. And he never wants to hear nothing at all about the children.

Al: Yes, well ... that is a bit odd. So, who's been teaching them up to now.

Miss T: It was a lady called Miss Jessel. But she died just a while ago. For the time being they're being looked after by Mrs Grose, the housekeeper. And of course, she's being helped by the cook and the gardener and the maid and the groom and...

Al: Wow! All *that* lot, just for a couple of rug rats!

Sounds like you've got it made m'dear. I'd go for it if I were you!

Miss T: Well, perhaps I will then ... I think?

12th June

Al: Hi there, all you lone cats. We've got Miss T on the line again. She says she needs to talk to someone. Well, that's *exactly* what the great Al Mighty's here for ... ha ha! So talk to me, baby! And how's the new job going, m'dear?

Miss T: Very nice thanks. Well ... *sort of.* The children are lovely. There's Miles, the little boy. He's just finished his first term at boarding school and he's a proper little gent. Ever so polite and bright as a button! Then there's his little sister, Flora. Such a *sweet* little thing! Both of them are quite, quite wonderful and I already love them to bits ... just like they were my *very* own. And they work *ever* so hard. Teaching them's a joy! So I suppose I  ought to be happy in my new post. The only thing is ... something a bit, er, *strange*, happened the other night.

Al: Tell us about it, m'dear... We're all ... ears!

Miss T: I'd just made sure the children were safely tucked up in bed and what with it being such a lovely evening I thought I'd take a stroll across the lawn. I hadn't gone more than a few steps when I looked up at the big tower at the end of the house and I saw a figure up there. It was a man. He was moving along and staring down at me. Then, the next moment, he disappeared!

Al: Well, I wouldn't worry about that, m'dear. He was probably just some passer-by having a snoop around.

Miss T: Yes, that's what I thought. But listen! Just as the man appeared all the rooks in the big trees next to the house stopped cawing! And, even though it was such a warm evening, the air around me went completely ... cold!

Al: Ooer! Hmm ... yes, I see what you mean. That *is* odd. Let's hope your imagination's not playing tricks on you, ha ha! Well, that's all we've got time for now, but keep us updated, won't you, Miss T?

16th June

Al: Hi, guys an' gals! And guess who's on the line ... again! Yes it's our very own Miss T, the lady with the mystery stranger. What's happened now, m'dear?

Miss T: Yesterday, me and Mrs Grose and the kiddies were just setting off for church when I suddenly remembered that I'd left my gloves in the schoolroom so I went back for them. Just as I was picking them up I got a shivery feeling so I looked up. And *guess* what I saw!

Al: What? What?

Miss T: There was this ... this ... face ... pressed up against the schoolroom window! It was *him*! The man

I'd seen on the tower. He was looking in ... all fierce and mad like! I rushed outside right away but he'd disappeared. Just like that! Then I bumped into Mrs Grose and she said that I looked as white as a sheet. So I told her what I'd seen and when I did *she* turned as white as a sheet too! 'Cos *she* knew something that *I* didn't!

Al: *What!?* What was it? Tell us, Miss T!

Miss T: I described the man to Mrs Grose and told her what a ... *horror* he was, then I said that his clothes looked like they didn't belong to him and, quick as a flash, *she* said, "That's 'cos they're ... *the master's*!" So right away I asked her if she knew the man and she said, "Yes, it's Quint. Peter Quint. He worked here. He wore the master's waistcoats after he'd gone to London. But then Mr Quint went away too."

And then I asked her where he'd gone and she said, "He's dead. Mr Quint is *dead*!"

Al: Ooer! Gordon Bennett! Cripes! And did she tell you *how* he died?

Miss T: Yes, she said he'd been found dead one winter's morning on the road from the village. He'd been in the pub and got drunk, then slipped on the ice and cracked his head. She said he were a bad'un. Always drinking and chattin' up women and whatnot, and really slimy and false with it, so the master didn't know what he was *really* like. And he was always hanging around little Miles. Trying to be his ... *pal*!

Al: Oooer! Well, I just don't know what to say to you, m'dear. But definitely keep in touch and let us know what else happens. It sounds like a *right* peculiar carry on!

10th August

Al: Hi, everyone. It's me, Al Mighty. And it's *her*! Miss T! She's on again. How's things, Miss T?

Miss T: Oh oh! Terrible! Just *terrible*! Oh! (*sob sob sob*)

Al: Oh no! What's happened now?

Miss T: Oh, lots and lots! A couple of weeks ago I took little Flora to the lake and we were sitting by it doing a geography lesson, pretending it was the Atlantic ocean. All of a sudden I saw this person on the other side of the water. It was a woman with an *awful* pale face ... all dressed in black. I recognized her straight away from a photograph Mrs Grose had shown me. It was the children's old teacher ... Miss Jessel!

Al: But *Miss T*! I thought that you said this Miss Jessel was d... Oooer! *Crikey*! I see what you mean!

Miss T: Yes! This horrible thing was staring straight at little Flora. And even though that lovely, lovely little girl had her back turned I just knew that Flora *knew* that *it* was there! And somehow I also knew ... (*sob sob*) ... that Miss Jessel ... (*sob*) ... had ... *come* ... for her!

Al: Oh no! That's *awful*! And what else has happened?

Miss T: Three or four nights ago I was sitting reading in bed when I got the feeling that something wasn't quite right in the house. I crept out of my room with a candle but as I started down the stairs it went out. That's when I saw him!

Al: What? Who?

Miss T: Peter Quint! The one I saw before. He was standing on the stairs *glaring* at me. My blood ran cold and I wanted to scream, but I didn't. I just stared back at him. Next moment he disappeared!

Al: Oh my goodness. You *are* having a ghastly time, aren't you!

Miss T: Wait, there's more! Last night I went to little Flora's room to check that she was all right. But when I got there, her bed was empty! I was beside myself with terror. And then I saw her, partly hidden by the curtains. But *she* didn't see *me*. She was looking out across the lawn. And I knew straight away that she was face to face with that horrible figure I'd seen by the lake.

Al: You mean Miss Jessel?

Miss T: Yes. And I also knew that she was somehow ... *communicating* with it.

Al: Which she hadn't been able to do before!?

Miss T: *Exactly*! But at that moment I didn't think about it any more. Because I'd just remembered little Miles! I knew that *someone* was prowling the grounds and I suddenly felt very, very frightened for him. As quickly and quietly as I could I slipped into the room next to Flora's and looked out of the window. What I saw made me shudder from head to toe. By the light of the moon I spied a figure standing on the lawn. It was looking up at the tower. Up above it on the tower was *another* figure which was looking straight down at it! And then I got the most terrible shock of all because ... I realized that the figure on the lawn was ... was...

Al: Yes? Was ... was...? Tell us *who* it was Miss T!

Miss T: It was little Miles!

Al: Oh my *good* night!

Miss T: The poor little thing seemed sort of ... sort of ... *spellbound* by what he was staring at.

Al: Which would be...?

Miss T: Peter Quint!

Al: Oh dear! The poor, poor little lad. What *ever* is going on up there, Miss T?

Miss T: I'm not ... entirely sure but ... but Mrs Grose has been telling me things that make me fear terribly for these poor children.

Al: What sort of things, Miss T?

Miss T: She says that when they were alive Mr Quint and Miss Jessel were sort of entangled! If you know what I mean?

Al: I think I do, Miss T. I think I do!

Miss T: She says that they were a most wicked and evil couple. And that they seemed to be with the children at every opportunity. Him with little Miles and her with Flora. She thinks they were intent on bringing these innocent little mites under their evil influence and doing them some terrible, terrible harm! So now I think ... I think ... that they've come back for them! And I believe they have it in their power to destroy my lovely, lovely little babies! Oh ... (*sob sob sob*)

Al: Oh no! That's really horrible! What ever can you do?

Miss T: So far, whenever I've seen those horrid apparitions they've always been at a distance from the children. It's as if they wish to get closer ... but can't! But I think it will only be a matter of time before they do!

Al: Have you talked to the children about them?

Miss T: No, I daren't! And the odd thing is, the children have never ever mentioned Miss Jessel, or Peter Quint. Not once! Which makes me even more suspicious and uneasy! Something awful and wicked and terrible is happening here. These poor little children are in the most dreadful danger. And I've just got to save them!

Al: But have you got a ghost of a chance, Miss T? Let's hope so! And please do keep your calls coming in. Me and the listeners are completely spellbound by your tale!

15th October

Al: Hello, everyone. I'm not taking any other calls this evening. The whole programme has been given over to poor Miss T. Compared to *her* worries you lots' troubles are *piffling*! Come on, Miss T. Let it all out, m'dear. You know a problem shared is a problem halved.

Miss T: Yes, yes, all right. Well, the other day little Miles came to me and asked me if I would like him to play the piano for me so I said I would. I listened to him for quite a while and then all of a sudden I realized that I hadn't seen little Flora for *ages*! I went to look for her but couldn't find her anywhere! I called Mrs Grose and we began to search the grounds of the house. When we got to the lake we saw that the boat was missing. We guessed she must have rowed herself to the other side so we belted around the lake shore like mad things and then...

Al: Yes! Yes! And *then*...?

Miss T: We found little Flora sitting on the grass, exactly where I thought she'd be. And as I went to speak to the poor little mite, sitting opposite her I saw ... I saw...

Al: *Miss Jessel?! Miss Jessel?!*

Miss T: *Yes!* She was sitting some distance away from Flora and staring straight at her. Exactly like before. I pointed the miserable, dreadful, horrible creature out to Mrs Grose but she said *she* couldn't see her! And Little Flora pretended that *she* couldn't see her either. But I knew different! *And* I said as much to Flora.

That's when she gave me that *look!*

Al: What look?

Miss T: It was a look that said she *hated* me. And that she was really, really angry with me for disturbing her. Mr M! I fear my lovely children are falling more and more under the spell of these hateful ghostly creatures! And what happened by the lake proves it, doesn't it?

Al: How do you mean?

Miss T: Well, the two of them cooked up a plan, didn't they? Miles played the piano to me just so's Flora could slip out and meet Miss Jessel! And ever since then Flora has been saying all sorts of wicked things about me. Mrs Grose has told me so! My lovely, lovely, sweet little girl doesn't like me any more and won't even be near me. Oh ... (*sob sob*). I fear they are both slipping away from me

Al: But you've just got to do something, Miss T! You can't let this happen!

Miss T: I know! I know! And I am! I've decided to send Flora away with Mrs Grose. They're leaving in a few days. I will stay here with Miles until it's time for him to return to school. *And*, even though I'm not supposed to get in touch with the children's uncle – the master, that is – I've written a letter to him telling him all that's going on! It's on the table in the hall right this moment, waiting for the groom to post it.

Al: Atta girl! That's the ticket! That should get a result! And don't forget! Al Mighty and all his listeners are following every twist and turn of your terrifying tale. So next time something happens ... just bell and tell!

16th November

Al: Stop what you're doing, everyone. Our very own Miss T's on the line. Now! She's says she got news and that's she's absolutely *desperate* to speak to us.

Miss T: Mr M! Oh, so much has happened since I last spoke to you. This phone call is *not* going to be easy. I'm in the dining room right now and I've asked little Miles to come and speak with me. You'll discover why quite soon! He'll be here in a moment. But my sweet, sweet little Flora ... is no longer with us!

Al: Oh no! Oh no! Has something *awful* happened to her?

Miss T: No, it isn't that! She has gone away with Mrs Grose, just as I intended.

Al: Phew, well ... *that's* a relief. And what about the letter you were going to send to the, er ... master? Did he get it?

Miss T: No, he didn't. And that is what I have to speak to Miles about.

Al: What do you mean?

Miss T: The letter was stolen from the hall table before it could be posted! Hush! Here he comes now. I'll put the telephone handset on the table next to us so that you may hear what I have to say to him. But what is this? Oh no! Oh no! OH NO!

Al: What is it, Miss T? What is it?

Miss T: *It's* there! At the window.

Al: Do you mean? Do you mean...?

Miss T: Yes, Quint is there! His awful face is pressed against the glass as I speak! It appeared the moment Miles entered the room. But my lovely boy hasn't seen it yet! I'll distract him from it! *And from this moment I must speak to you in whispers, Mr M! I think he is too young to understand what I am doing.*

Al: *Yes! Yes! Do that, Miss T. Do that! We're all rooting for you!*

Miles: Hello, Miss T. This is a late time to be asking me questions.

Miss T: Yes, my dear, I know. But this is very, very important! Now please look at me, Miles. No, don't turn round! *Whatever you do, don't turn round!* That's it! Good boy! Now, I'm going to ask you a question. It's about the letter I left on the table in the hall. The one the groom was supposed to post to your uncle. *Oh my goodness gracious, Mr M. The face at the window. It has turned furious! It's glaring like a mad thing again! I feel like I am fighting to save the little soul of this child from a ... demon! I must hurry.*

Al: *Yes! Yes! Do that, Miss T. Do that!*

Miss T: Miles, my dear, did you take that letter?

Miles: Yes, I did. And I am very sorry that I did, Miss T. But I wanted to know what you said about me.

Miss T: Oh, my dear, dear child. I am so glad that you told me that! Come, let me hug you! *Mr M, I am squeezing him with all my might. He must not turn round! But that thing is still glaring in. It is more furious than ever! NO! I cannot stand it any longer! It is driving me mad! LEAVE US ALONE WILL YOU! GET AWAY FROM THAT WINDOW ... YOU ... MONSTER!*

Miles: What is it, Miss T? What is it? Is *she* here?

Miss T: Who do you mean, my dear?

Miles: Miss Jessel! Miss Jessel! Of course!

Miss T: No, my dear. It's *not* Miss Jessel. But yes, *it* is there!

Al: *Don't let him turn round, Miss T. Don't let him turn round!*

Miles: But ... is it ... is it ... him?

Miss T: Who do you mean, my dear?

Miles: Peter Quint ... you *devil*! Where *is* he?

Al: *Keep your arms around him, Miss T! Keep your arms around him!*

Miss T: Hush, dear Miles. It doesn't matter. He's lost you now. He can't hurt you any more. *Oh no, Mr M. Miles is suddenly white with anger. He is sniffing the air like a little dog and jerking around in my arms, and jerking around ... OH NO!*

Al: Miss T! Miss T! What's the matter? What *ever* is the matter? FOR CRYING OUT LOUD, MISS T! *TELL US* WHAT'S THE MATTER!

Miss T: Oh, oh, oh. My poor, poor, poor little boy is lying here in my arms. And, Mr Al, his little heart ... has stopped! Mr Al, he is *gone*! And so too, is Peter Quint.

Al: Oh no! Oh no! Oh no! That's terrible, terrible, terrible. Oh, oh, oh... I just can't go on with the show. I really can't! (*sob sob sob*) I feel *awful*. I'm sorry everyone. I just need to go and find someone to talk to about this ... (*sob ... sob ... sob*)

The faint-spirits' guide to avoiding ghosts

What a pity that poor woman didn't get some expert advice about dealing with ghosts. Then things might have turned out quite differently. Well, at least you'll have no excuse for being caught out by the spooks, not when you've read the things you can do to keep ghosts away…

Wear an amulet
Warning! This is the jewellery kind of amulet, not the egg and mushroom sort. Wear it on your wrist, neck or head … or boys, if you're bothered about being teased about that rather fetching diamond tiara, just bung it in your pocket. Amulets are made from precious or odd-shaped stones which are thought to have supernatural powers. They scare ghosts to death!

Carry some salt around in your pocket
Salt has always been associated with keeping away spooks and evil spirits and bringing good luck, though no one's sure why. So, as well as carting a couple of tons around in your pocket, throw a pinch over your left shoulder. You should also scatter some on your front doorstep.

Nature note: Some cruel and short-sighted people even say that salt is also brilliant for reducing phantom slugs to little puddles of ectoplasm.

Get some help out of doors

When you go through a door, don't just shut it behind you like you normally never do, but slam it lots of times. If you are being followed by a ghost this trick will catch it out and no doubt cause it a great deal of pain, inconvenience and confusion, especially if it's an extra-dim ghost. However, if you're entering a shop and are being followed by several other shoppers this cunning ruse may just cause *you* a great deal of embarrassment.

In Norfolk some people actually go to the trouble of turning doors round on their hinges to fool the ghosts. They must all be really thick in Norfolk (the ghosts, not the people)!

Be on your "metal"

Sometimes it takes nerves of steel and an iron will to beat the more determined sort of ghost, so here are a few tips from days gone by.

a) If you know where your ghost is coming from place an iron rod on its grave. This is said to stop it from "rising" (and also gives it bruises the size of hens' eggs).

b) Place an iron horseshoe on your front door. Horseshoes are generally thought to keep away spooks. This has never been proved scientifically. Nevertheless, when asked if they've ever been troubled by ghosts nine out of ten horses said, "Neigh!"

c) Carrying some nails around in your pocket is said to keep ghosts away.

Pins stuck in gate posts and front doors are also said to do the trick.

Get some help from rosemary

This is the herb not the girl (she's frightened of her own shadow!). If you put some rosemary near your front and back doors you will never be troubled by ghosts (but tough luck if you've got a side door). If the rosemary doesn't work you could always try a yellow flower called St John's Wort. People on the Isle of Wight believe that if you step on a bit of it a fairy horse appears beneath you and takes you away for an entire night (then the following night a man in a white coat appears and takes you away for ever!).

Exorcise your ghost

Do this by running away from it as fast as you can so that it chases after you. If the ghost hasn't been exorcised regularly it will be listless, flabby and lethargic. In no time at all it will be on its knees gasping for breath and complaining of the stitch. Now go back and give it a punch in the gob. No ... wait a minute! That's a load of cobbledespook! The proper way to "exorcise" a ghost (rather than "exercise" it) is to call in a priest or vicar and get them to say a few prayers at it.

Important note: This method of ghost eradication will only work for people who believe in the Christian religion *and* believe in ghosts.

Draw a chalk circle or a star shape around yourself
It's said that ghosts are unable to step inside these shapes. So as long as you stand absolutely still you'll be OK. However, if you actually want to *go* somewhere you're going to have to draw a *really BIG* circle or star (recommended diameter 5,000 kilometres). Either that, or just draw it again, and again ... and again!

As a last resort you could get yourself a Hula-Hoop (the star-shaped ones aren't quite as easy to come by as they used to be).

Try a "global" remedy
You could try what the Algonquin Indians of Canada did and leave out food for ghosts to keep them from haunting. Of course, if you do this at Christmas you're going to have to put out double the snacks. Some for the spooks and some for Santa! In China, people burn incense sticks to frighten away ghosts. (Incense smells quite nice, so wouldn't this attract them?) They also bang drums and set off fireworks at funerals to frighten away ghosts. The 5 November "Guy Fawkes' night" firework and bonfire celebrations held in Britain are linked to earlier ghost-scaring rituals. And what a coincidence that they take place so near to Hallowe'en! The onset of the dark cold nights in autumn have

always been associated with the arrival of spooks and evil spirits.

Jump or step over a broom
It's said this is an excellent way of avoiding an unpleasant brush with a spook (although some of you may consider this to be rather a sweeping statement). Taking a broom to bed with you is also thought to ward off ghosts. No cheating though, vacuum cleaners don't count!

Do it nature's way
Here's a round-up of some other things that ghosts are said to "have a problem with". They're all natural, old-fashioned ghost deterrents that won't cost you a bean. In the old days most folk were poorer than church mice and couldn't just nip down to the local spooker-market and buy a can of ghost-repellant spray like we all can nowadays. What do you mean, you've never heard of it – you're obviously shopping at the wrong places.

Oak leaves
Hang them above your bed – but remember, if they fall down during the night and frighten you out of your skin ... the oaks on you! (What acorny quip.)

Palm leaves
Make them into the shape of a cross (then use it to belt the living daylights out of the ghost!).

Rowan tree berries
Wear them as a necklace – they're deadly poisonous so don't be tempted to nibble them (but by all means feed them to the ghost!).

Birch tree twigs
You're supposed to carry them in your pocket or even wear them! (Maybe as a fright twig? Ha ha!)

Word of warning: With this lot surrounding you, no way are you going to be troubled by ghosts ... however, you will receive frequent visits from groups of nature ramblers and nesting birds.

On the Brighton Road

Imagine meeting a ghost and chatting to it, but not actually *realizing* that it *was* a ghost! The next tale in our spooky line-up is about just such a meeting. And what makes it even *more* intriguing is that we aren't even sure that the man who meets the ghost isn't already a ghost himself! Richard Middleton (1882–1911), the author of the story, deliberately weaves all sorts of clues and false trails into his tale to keep us guessing about his two main characters. And that makes us ask other questions too. Like, if you do become a ghost, how do you *know* you're one? Do you get a letter of appointment from the spooksman-in-chief? Or does it just gradually "dawn" on you, especially when your friends react rather oddly whenever you pop in to see them?

"On the Brighton Road" (1912) is set in England in the early 1900s. At that time it was common to see tramps walking countryside lanes and roads. These "gentlemen of the road", as they were known, more or less wandered as they pleased, were given food at farms and cottages, and slept in barns or fields. Sounds like a great adventure, doesn't it? But it wasn't! All sorts of bad things happened to the tramps, including death from starvation, cold ... and worse! So, if there are such things as ghosts, it seems likely that at *least* one tramp would end up as a spook. Or maybe even two?

Richard's short story is perfect material for an "old-fashioned" black and white spook movie. Preferably with lots of bleak winter scenery, creepy violins and "moody" and atmospheric camera shots. So, dim the lights, sit back with the script and let your imagination roll out the "chilling" pictures. Maybe you'll manage to work out just how many ghosts there are in this story. And just who's fooling who!

Fellow traveller

Tramp (*slowly getting to his feet, beginning to talk to himself*):

Uh, oh ... I was so lovely and warm down there. I might have been in my old bed for all I knew! (*Bats snow off himself and shakes arms.*) And, all things considered, I definitely don't feel too bad at all. What with it being so cold last night I suppose I'm lucky to have even *woken* up! (*Shivers.*) Or *un*lucky, maybe? This tramping life certainly isn't much to wake up to. (*He begins to walk along the road in the direction of London.*) Now? What did I do yesterday? I walked until I was done for ... that's what! And I'm *still* only twelve miles from Brighton! Bloomin' snow! Bloomin' Brighton! Bloomin' *everything*!

Tramp: I really don't know whether to be pleased that it was only the sleep that took me last night. And not the other thing? Or should I be sorry? I dunno! Glad? Sorry? Glad? Oh, who cares!

Boy: You on the road then, guv'nor, same as me?

Tramp: I think I am.

Boy (*catching up with tramp and limping along at the side of him*): The road's a bit lonely this early in the day, ain't it mate? I'll walk a bit of the way wiv yer then, if yer don't mind. As long as yer don't walk too fast.

Tramp: That's fine by me. I'll be glad of the company.

Boy: I'm eighteen yer know. Bet you thought I was younger!

Tramp: I'd have said fourteen or fifteen.

Boy: Well, yer'd have been wrong! I were eighteen last summer. I been on the road for six years now, yer know! I kept runnin' away from home when I were a nipper! An' the cops kept draggin' me back. They were good to me, them cops were. But now I ain't got no home to run away from.

Tramp: Nor me.

Boy: Yes, but you *have* had, ain't yer? I can tell that *you've* been a gentleman what's 'ad a bit of bad luck an' come down a bit in the world. Yer've had a nice home an' a decent life, ain't yer? An' that probably makes this trampin' life much harder for you than for the likes of me, don't it?

Tramp: I suppose you could say that. I certainly haven't been on the road for anywhere near as long as you have.

Boy: I can tell that from the way yer walkin'. You've not got the tiredness yet, 'ave yer? Yer've still got a bit of a spring in yer step! Maybe you're hopin' to get to somethin' when you get to the other end?

Tramp (*sadly*): I'm not so sure about that. (*Pauses.*) Well yes, I suppose I'm always expecting *something* to turn up.

Boy (*laughs bitterly*): Ha! You'll soon grow out of *that*. Ah well, at least you'll find it's a bit *warmer* in London than round here. What with all the buildin's an' that. But I'm tellin' yer mate! There ain't much grub to be had up there.

Tramp (*with sadness*): I was hoping I'd maybe meet someone who'll understand and help me to...

Boy (*interrupting*): These country people are loads better than the London folk. Last night I slept in a barn with the cows. Nice an' warm an' comfy it was too. An' this mornin' the farmer found me! But he didn't boot me out. What with me bein' so small an' skinny an' all he took pity on me an' gave me a cuppa tea an' a slice of toast. Which is better than what they do for you in London, I can tell yer mate. Up there, they just gives yer a bowl of soup up on the Embankment, an' that's yer lot! An' after that, it's the coppers movin' yer on all the time. You never gets a moment's rest. Not never! It's the tiredness what's worse!

Tramp (*nodding enthusiastically*): Yes, I know *exactly* what you mean! Do you know, last night I was *so* tired that I just dropped down at the side of the road and slept where I'd fallen. It's a wonder I didn't die what with it being so freezing cold.

Boy (*giving tramp a very strange look*): But how do you know you didn't?

Tramp (*suddenly looking puzzled and slightly alarmed*): Didn't *what*?!

Boy: Die ... of course! I mean, how do you know that you're *not* dead?

Tramp (*nervously*): I'm not sure that I understand you.

Boy (*in a hoarse whisper*): Listen, mate! *Us* sort of folk can't *never* get away from this sort of thing. And even if we *want* to, we *can't*, you know! Always bein' hungry an' thirsty. An' bein' dog tired out an' *walkin'* ... *walkin'* ... *walkin'*! It's with us sorts for *ever*. An' if someone does ever offer me a bit of work an' a roof over my head I get this sick feelin' deep down inside me. Now! Do you think I look strong? Yes! I know I'm little for my age, but I've been goin' around

like this for six years you know! An' do you *really* fink that I'm *not* dead!? Why, I was drownded while I was swimmin' in the sea off Brighton beach. An' I was killed by a gypsy. He got me with this big rusty spike. Split my head like a rotten spud, he did. An' *twice* I been frozen up. Just like *you* was last night! And I were knocked down by a motor car. On this very road! But still I'm walkin' along it, ain't I? I ain't got no choice, mate! I just can't 'elp it! I *'ave* to do it! Dead! I'm telling yer ... the likes of you ... and me, we can't *never* get away from it! Not never! (*Violent coughing.*)

Tramp: Here, son, take my coat...

Boy (*collapsing to hands and knees in the snow and wretching violently*): Haaaa haaa... *Keep* yer rotten coat, will yer! I tell yer, I'm all right! Wasn't yer listenin' to *nothin'* what I said! I was tellin' yer about the road! I can see yer've not got the idea proper yet, 'ave yer! But yer will! Yer will! An' then yer'll know soon enough what I'm talkin' about! I'm tellin' yer! We're *all* dead! *All* of us what's on the road! An' we're all tired as tired can be. But somehow we just can't *ever* leave it! (*He pauses for a moment then, with the aid of the tramp, he staggers back to his feet.*) But I suppose it's all right sometimes. Like in the summer when there's all them nice smells of hay and that. An' there's wakin' up on a spring mornin' with the birds all singin'...

Boy (*whispering, hardly audible*): I'm sick, yer know ... real sick...

Car driver: What's the problem? Can I be of any help?
Tramp: It's this boy. He's in a bad way.
Car driver: I'm a doctor. Help me get him in the back of my car and I'll take a look at him!

Car driver (*looking very grave and shaking head*): He really is in a bad way, isn't he? It's the final stages of pneumonia. I'll take him straight to the hospital at Crawley. But I think I'm probably already too late. Can I offer you a lift too?
Tramp: No, no thanks!

Boy (*whispering, hardly audible above the car's engine starting up*): I'll meet yer at Reigate then. Then you'll see! (*He winks again as the car draws away, leaving the tramp with a horrified and confused look on his face.*)

Tramp: Not too far to go now. And at least I got that crust of bread at the cottage and the sleep in the barn. Now! Hang on! What's that?

Boy: On the road are you, guvnor? Same as me? Well, if you don't mind, I'll think I'll walk a bit of the way with you. Just as long as you don't walk too fast! The road's a bit lonely around this time of day, ain't it, mate?

Tramp (*aghast*): You! But ... but ... what about the pneumonia?

Boy: I died at Crawley this morning.

Terrifying travellers

Richard's tale is made up but there are masses of people around who reckon they've met phantom travellers while they've been out and about. Here's a bus stop's worth for you to be going home with...

The phantom hitch-hiker of Totternoe

A man called Roy Fulton was driving home from the pub when he saw a young chap thumbing a lift so he stopped and said, "I'm going towards Dunstable." The young bloke said nothing but got into the front seat of Roy's van, then pointed to a signpost that said, "Totternoe Village". As Roy drove towards the village at a steady 45 miles an hour he reached into his pocket and pulled out a packet of cigarettes. He got one out and said to the young man, "Cigarette?" But the young man didn't take the fag. Because he was no longer in the van! Roy reached out and felt the seat next to him. It was still warm! Ooer!

Important points: This is what is known as a variation of "the classic hitch-hiker story", so it's a bit suspect, and if the bloke was a ghost, why did he have a warm bum?

The woman in black (who haunts the rail track)

Sometime around the year 1900 a man called Colonel Ewart was travelling to London by train. He decided to have a bit of a snooze in his empty railway carriage. When he awoke he was surprised to see a veiled woman dressed in black sitting opposite him. She was rocking backwards and forwards and singing a lullaby to some "*thing*" in her lap. The colonel was puzzled by this because there didn't actually seem to be anything there (maybe she was just extremely fond of her lap?). At that moment the train screeched to a halt and ... BONK KERDUMPH! ... poor Colonel Ewart was knocked unconscious by a flying suitcase. When he regained consciousness the weird woman had disappeared.

As soon as he arrived in London the colonel questioned a railway porter about his mysterious travelling companion. What the porter told the colonel was this...

Many years before, a young bride had been travelling on the train with her new husband. In order to get a really good shufti at the passing countryside the bridegroom opened the window and stuck his head out – not really a good idea on a speeding train. Some moments later the young bloke's neck came into contact with a wire at the side of the track. The wire stayed where it was but the fellah's head dropped to the ground, having been sliced off at the neck! His decapitated body then toppled backwards – straight into the lap of his new bride. UUUURGH! When the train got to London the poor girl was found cradling the headless corpse and singing a lullaby to it. Yes! The shock of the horrible experience had sent her completely off the rails. She stayed like that until she died a few months later.

The spitting image of the Delamere Forest

Mr Pressick was driving his car along a country lane near the Delamere Forest in Cheshire when he got lost, so he slowed down to ask directions of a man who was walking his dog. Suddenly Mr Pressick noticed that although it was a perfectly still and windless night the man was bent over as if he was walking into a howling gale and the dribble of spit dangling from the dog's mouth was blowing backwards! Mr Pressick was gob-smacked by this amazing phenomenon but nevertheless he stopped and asked him for directions. Neither the man nor the dog said a word and moments later they both vanished! Some time later a farmer told Mr Pressick that a man and his dog had been killed on that very lane one dark and stormy night!

The lost case of the phantom flier

In 1948 a Sabena Airlines plane crashed in fog at Heathrow Airport and all 20 people on board were killed. As the rescue services picked through the smoking wreckage, a ghostly figure stepped out of the mist and said, "Excuse me have you found my brief-case?" then disappeared before the searchers had time to answer. It's generally believed that the person was the ghost of one of the crash victims. He's since been seen walking next to the runway where the crash took place and is no doubt still feeling dead upset about his lost luggage (along with about 20,000 other airline travellers).

Madame Pele

This spook is regularly seen walking or standing at the side of roads on the island of Hawaii and often has a small white dog with her. It's not a good idea to give her a lift because she's in charge of all the local volcanoes and as a way of expressing her deep gratitude she'll make sure you get killed the very next time one blows its top. In order to keep the cantankerous old "lava-lout" happy the local people leave her roast chickens around the rim of the volcanoes.

Resurrection Mary ... pretty scary!

Mary lived in Chicago in the USA and was crazy about dancing. One night in 1934 she was killed in a car accident after an evening's dancing. Not long after her death, people driving their cars through Chicago reported how a beautiful blonde woman dressed in white had leapt on to their running boards and asked them to give her a lift to her favourite dance hall.

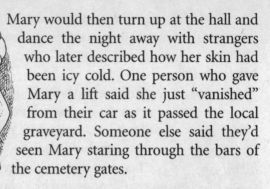

Mary would then turn up at the hall and dance the night away with strangers who later described how her skin had been icy cold. One person who gave Mary a lift said she just "vanished" from their car as it passed the local graveyard. Someone else said they'd seen Mary staring through the bars of the cemetery gates.

The pillion passenger of the Blackwall Tunnel

A motorcyclist was brumming along the road that leads to the Blackwall Tunnel (the one that goes under the River Thames in London). Seeing a hitch-hiker standing by the roadside he stopped and gave him a lift. A few minutes later he zoomed through the tunnel but when he came out the other side his passenger had disappeared! "Ooh cripes!" thought the motorcyclist, "The twit's gone and fallen off in the tunnel. I'll have to go back and look for him!" So he did, but he couldn't find him anywhere! The next day the motorcyclist visited the address the hitch-hiker had given him. When he described his passenger to the people who lived there they told him that the man had died many years before (not surprising really in view of his inability to stay on motorbikes).

Useful note: This is another variation of "the classic phantom hitch-hiker story".

The stupid spook of the Stockbridge Bypass

On the Stockbridge bypass near Sheffield there is said to be a ghost who jumps out at passing cars. It's supposed to have caused a total of 57 crashes. A policeman called Dick was called to investigate a strange figure hovering above the road. Later on Dick said, "I saw it next to my panda and then something banged my head." That's a bit hard to swallow, isn't it? Especially coming from a man who takes cuddly toys out on patrol with him!

The phantom hitch-hiker of Ragley Hall

A man was driving his car past Ragley Hall in Warwickshire, late one night when his car headlights picked out a shrivelled old fig lurking in a tree. As he got nearer he was horrified to see the fig leap out of the tree then dangle in mid-air, as if suspended by a rope! Ooer! The man immediately thought he'd witnessed a suicide, but when he got out of his car to investigate the fig had disappeared. (Oops sorry, this should be *figure* – not fig!) One year later, on exactly the same date (yes, it's definitely date!), he saw the figure again and the following night his wife saw it too, but this time it was thumbing a lift. (What an incredibly indecisive ghost!) After this, other motorists came forward and described how they'd picked up an old woman hitch-hiker at the gates of Ragley Hall but had later "lost" her after she'd mysteriously disappeared from the back seat of their car. After an investigation of the area the skeleton of an old woman was found buried by the roadside. No one has ever been able to come up with a good raisin for any of these strange occurrences!

Tragic Kate (who was extremely ... late!)
Back in the seventeenth century Alexander Oatway and his son William liked to play with boats. But not at the local boating lake. Their idea of fun was to stand on the seashore near Ilfracombe in Devon and wave lights at passing ships in order to lure them on to the rocks there. Once a boat was well and truly pranged and the crew all drowned, Al and Will would steal the ship's goodies.

When William grew up, he and his wife carried on the family shipwrecking business from Chambercombe Manor, the house that had been built with the profits. One evening, as they were plundering a wreck, they found one of the ship's passengers lying on the beach. It was a young woman who was still alive but was so bashed up by the angry seas and the jagged rocks that she was completely unrecognizable. They carried her back to the manor house but she died during the night. "Ah well! Waste not! Want not!" said the greedy Oatways and they swiped the girl's dosh and trinkets, then buried her body.

A few days later the shipping authorities arrived to investigate the wreck and recover the bodies. They checked the passenger list and announced that the only person not accounted for was a ... Kate Oatway!

Yes, the girl the Oatways had murdered and robbed was their own daughter who, unbeknownst to them, had been travelling to England from Dublin, where she'd moved some years before! The Oatways were devastated and so was Kate. Her ghost began to haunt Chalcombe Manor so regularly that Mum and Dad left the place and never returned. More than a hundred years later a skeleton, thought to be Kate's, was discovered at the Manor. It was removed to a proper grave in the hope that her ghost would settle down a bit. But it didn't. According to local legend, it's still in there moaning and groaning about the rotten deal it got from its horrible mum and dad. And can you *blame* it!

Oh, Whistle and I'll Come to You, My Lad

Some people think that objects and places sort of "hold" spirits and it only needs someone to come along and do something that disturbs those spirits for some serious haunting to start. Even though they may have lain undisturbed for hundreds of years! That's more or less what happens in "Whistle and I'll Come to You My Lad" (1904) by M R James (1862–1936). It all starts innocently enough with a university professor having a nice holiday at the seaside. But being an inquisitive type he starts to nose around and eventually discovers something *very* old and *very* interesting. His "find", and what he does with it, sets off a chain of events that eventually leads to him having an experience so awful that he will never ever completely recover from it. When you've read his letters to his chums in Cambridge perhaps you'll think twice next time you fancy digging in the sand!

Wish you were here

The Globe Hotel,
Burnstow, Suffolk.

12th June

To all my friends in the staffroom,
St James College,
Cambridge.

Dear chums,
I arrived at Burnstow yesterday. It's a lovely, lovely little place, and not at all busy, with a great feeling of history everywhere. I've got a large room at the Globe Inn, which is on the village green. There's even a spare bed in it! So why don't you pop down and join me if you get a chance? You're most welcome! There's a great view out to sea from my main window and I can see up and down the seashore from the smaller ones at the side. The golf course looks superb and I'm planning to be on it every single day. I've also brought lots of books down with me as I'm going to try and do a bit of work. Yes, I really am!
Your dear old friend,

Professor Parkins

PS I'm finding it a bit difficult getting used to being retired, so I'll write every day if it's all the same to you fellows! I hope you don't mind, but you know what a scribbler I am!

14th June

Hello there chaps,

I've had a most interesting day! I spent most of it playing golf with a retired military chap called Colonel Wilson. He's a very decent sort (if a bit fierce!) and he's also staying at the Globe. After my day's golf I decided to walk back to the hotel on my own as I was quite taken with the idea of exploring the beach. I was making my way across the rough ground between the golf course and the sand dunes when I tripped over a big stone. I glanced down at it and realized that I must be crossing the site of the abandoned medieval church I'd been told about so I thought I'd take a poke around. I spotted that a patch of grass had been dug away by a rabbit or something and thought that would be an excellent place to start. I took out my knife and began scraping away to see what I could come up with. As I chipped at the earth some rock suddenly crumbled away and I found what looked like a little hidey-hole in between the old foundation stones. Most interesting! It probably hadn't been disturbed for centuries! As I withdrew my knife I thought I heard a faint clink of metal so I put my hand inside and began fishing around. A moment later my fingers rested on what felt like a metal tube. I pulled it out and took a quick look at it. It was caked in muck so I couldn't really tell what it was. At that moment my stomach began rumbling and reminded me it was dinnertime so I dropped the thingamajig in my pocket and set off at a brisk trot.

I'd been jogging for about five minutes when I glanced over my shoulder to see how far I'd come along the beach and noticed a figure some distance behind me. Whoever it was seemed to be trying to catch up with me. Well, to be quite honest with you, I didn't really feel like waiting for them, whoever they were! Especially as I was already late for dinner. As it was, I only just arrived in time!

After dinner I spent a challenging hour or so playing chess with Colonel Wilson. This really is turning out to be the most pleasant of hols!

Toodle pip old things,

The Professor

16th June

Dear friends,

Hello again. Another great day's golf today. I beat the Colonel by six shots and finished with a birdie on the eighteenth! Boy, was he miffed! This evening as I was returning to my room quite late one of the maids stopped me and handed me something. It was the metal thingamajig I told you about in my last letter, the one I'd found at the ruins. Apparently it had fallen out of my coat pocket when she was giving it a brush down. Silly old me had forgotten all about it! Anyway, having nothing better to do, I took it back to my room and gave it a thorough clean with my penknife. Once I'd scraped all the muck away I could see that it was some sort of whistle! And a very ancient one at that! And now I'd made it as clean as a whistle! Ha ha! Being the old fusspot that I am, I scraped the muck onto a piece of paper and emptied it out of the window. Just as I was doing this I spied a figure on the beach below. It gave me quite a shock actually. Well, it was a quarter to midnight. Why ever would anyone want to be on the sands at that time of night? Some of these Burnstow people do keep late hours!

As soon as I'd got rid of the mess I went back to examining my find. I could now make out that the words "FUR FLA BIS FLE QUIS EST ESTE QUI VENIT" had been engraved upon the metal. My Latin's not as hot as it used to be, so I'm not entirely sure what they meant, but I knew it was something like "Who is this coming?" "Well!" I thought, "the best way to find out is probably to blow the blooming thing." So I did! The sound it made was rather soft and pleasant, the kind that brings pictures to your mind, just as some smells do! The image that immediately came into my head was of a person wandering around on a dark and windy night. I thought I'd blow again to see what else I could see. This time I got no picture, but the strangest thing did happen – although I'm sure it was a coincidence! About a second after I'd blown the whistle the wildest wind began to howl through my bedroom window which still happened to be open. It took me all my strength to shut it again. Then, a minute or so later, just as quickly as it had risen, the wind dropped.

So what do you make of all that then? I know, don't tell me! You probably think it's just a silly old duffer letting his imagination get the better of him, don't you!

All the best,

Professor Parkins

19th June

Dear chaps,

How are things with you? Yesterday I had another most exhausting and enjoyable day's golf. It really did leave me feeling quite drained! However, when I turned in for the night, for some reason, I just couldn't manage to nod off. I've no idea why! So I had no choice but to lay there listening to my heart beating and thinking about the events of my day.

Now! Do you ever get that thing when you close your eyes and a sort of film begins to play on the back of your eyelids? Well, that's just what happened to me the moment I closed mine. The scene that appeared to me was a beach exactly like the one outside my bedroom window. All the way along it were those things they call groynes. You know, the wooden barriers they build to stop the tide from shifting the sand. Exactly like they've got here at Burnstow!

In the far distance I could see a black object bobbing up and down. As it came nearer I realized it was a man running along the beach. Every now and again he would have to stop and clamber over one of these wooden groynes. And each one he climbed appeared to make him more tired. Finally, all the running and climbing seemed to get too much for him. He almost fell over a groyne, then lay behind it, as if completely exhausted. Even though I couldn't see his face I had the distinct feeling that he was desperately, desperately frightened of something! Then I noticed a patch of light moving to and fro in the distance. A pale figure was approaching him at the most alarming speed. Not in a straight line, but zigzagging all over the beach. Occasionally it would run to the water's edge, stoop down for a moment, as if to sniff the water or sand, then leap up again and continue its headlong dash. At last it reached a spot just metres from the wooden barrier which the man was hiding behind. And then it stopped quite suddenly, raised its arms above its head for a moment, and dashed straight towards the chap behind the groyne! I'm sorry to tell you that at this point I was unable to keep my eyes closed any longer. And of course, the moment I opened them, my "film" was gone! To be quite honest with you I found the whole thing rather disturbing ... if not to say a little frightening! However, I did finally manage to drift off to sleep after reading for a while.

All the best,

Parky

22nd June

Hello there you fellows,

This hol' of mine is turning out to be far more interesting than I ever expected it to be! Some really odd and intriguing things have happened today. And one or two of them have sent a few rather unwelcome shivers down my spine!

This morning, after eating a hearty breakfast of eggs and bacon, I returned to my bedroom to prepare for another day's golf. Just as I was zipping up my golf bag I heard a tap on the bedroom door. It was the chambermaid. She asked me if I would like any extra blankets as the weather had turned a bit chillier. So I told her to go ahead and do as she saw fit. She hesitated for a moment and asked if she should put the blankets on both of the beds. This puzzled me somewhat as I'd only actually slept in one of them, so I told her so.

"Well, sir," she replied. "We definitely 'ad to make up the two of them this mornin'! They was both quite rumpled. We thought as you'd probably tried the both of them."

This did make me wonder for a moment but then I realized that I'd probably put my luggage down on the spare bed and that's what had rumpled its sheets. I told her so, then thought no more of the matter. Fifteen minutes later I set off for my round of golf with the Colonel.

After the game the Colonel and I strolled back together. We'd almost reached the front door of the hotel when this young chap suddenly came racing round the corner of the building and crashed headlong into the Colonel, almost knocking him over!

"I say! Steady on, young fellow!" he barked. "Whatever is the matter with you?"

"I seen it! I seen it!" blurted out the boy, who looked so upset that I thought he might collapse at our feet!

"Seen it?" I said.

"Yes yes!" panted the boy. "It ... it ... it ... w-w-waved at me! Out the w-w-window! An' I don't like it! I don't like it!"

"What window?" said the Colonel. "What on earth are you talking about, lad?"

"I was playin' on the grass wiv me mates," gasped the boy, "and I looked up at that window and there was this ... this ... thing at it! All pale an' white it was. An' it ... an' it ... waved at me."

"Well, did you see its face?" I said.

"No ... I d-d-didn't!" cried the boy. It ... d-d-didn't 'ave one!" And then he began to gibber like a lunatic and tremble all over.

"Point to the window it was at!" said the Colonel. The boy reluctantly raised his arm and

indicated a spot on the front of the hotel. He was pointing to the window of my bedroom!

After telling the lad that there was probably absolutely nothing to worry about, the Colonel gave him a sixpence, then we hurried up to my room. The door was still locked so I found my key and let us in.

"Well, nothing seems to have been disturbed," I said, looking around.

"Apart from your bed!" said the Colonel.

"No, that's not my bed," I said. "I sleep in the other one. But you're right. It does look as though someone's slept in that one too."

We both paused for a moment, each thinking about this strange turn of events and trying to make sense of it. Then the Colonel said, "I suppose what the lad saw could have been the maid making up the bed? And then maybe she was called away before she'd finished? You know how these silly schoolboys can get carried away by their over-active imaginations."

"Yes!" I said. "That's most probably the most likely explanation." Although I did think to myself that that would be rather odd as she'd already made up the bed this morning!

Well, chaps, that was all a few hours ago. Since then I've had dinner and now I'm sitting at the table typing you this letter. I'm sure I've nothing to worry about but to be quite honest with you, I do feel a bit nervous about going to bed tonight.

Yes! I know what you're thinking: "Silly old duffer, Parky! Getting all of a twitter over nothing!"

Ah well, fingers crossed. Let's hope I have a peaceful night! At least the Colonel's said he'll be on standby if I should need him. And that's reassuring to know! Nighty night.

Your old pal,

Parky

The Willows,
Trinity Road,
Cambridge.

24th October

Dear colleagues,

You are, no doubt, wondering why you have not heard from me in such a long time. You may have heard rumours that I returned quite suddenly from my holiday at Burnstow earlier in the summer and that since then I have remained here in my house in Cambridge, seeing no one and receiving no visitors apart from my housekeeper. Well, the rumours are correct. I will now attempt to explain my sudden return from my holiday and my failure to make contact with any of you.

It all results from the events that took place on the terrible night of the 22nd June. So dreadful were they and such was the devastating effect they had upon me that this is the first time I have actually been able to put pen to paper.

I will now return to the events of that fateful evening. After finishing my letter (the one you probably received on or about the 24th June) I took it to reception for posting, then prepared myself for bed. As I did, I noticed that there was a full moon. It occurred to me that as there were no curtains at the main window of my room the moonlight would be streaming directly on to my face and possibly keeping me awake. In order to prevent this I took my travelling rug from my suitcase and, with the help of a few safety pins, a stick and my umbrella, I rigged up a sort of screen. I then got into bed and soon drifted into a deep and peaceful sleep.

I must have been asleep for a couple of hours when I was awoken by a sharp rattling and clattering sound. I opened my eyes and immediately saw that my screen had collapsed and that the moonlight was now flooding into the room! As I lay there wondering whether I could be bothered to get out of bed and repair the screen, I suddenly heard a noise from the spare bed next to me. It sounded like a mouse, so I wasn't too alarmed. But then I heard it again. It was much much louder this time and I realized that this was far more noise than any mouse could possibly make. I was just preparing myself to get out of bed and investigate when something happened which was so utterly, utterly terrifying that I will remember it for the rest of my days.

As I glanced towards the spare bed, I suddenly saw a figure sit up in it! Fear of a sort that I have never felt before in my entire life engulfed my whole being. The hairs on the back of my neck rose as one and in just moments a gut-wrenching terror had turned my insides to water! Without thinking, I leapt from my bed and seized the stick that had been holding up the screen. This was the very worst thing I could possibly have done! For as I got up, the figure slid from the bed and positioned itself between me and the door of my room. It then stood with its arms outspread, blocking my escape route completely! I dared not push past it for I could not bear to touch it. I do not know why! And I feared that my end was near!

However, at that moment, the thing stooped, ran towards my bed and began feeling and ... sniffing ... the pillows! With a mixture of relief and horror I suddenly realized that it, whatever it was, was blind! I took my chance, dashed to the window and flung it open in readiness to make my escape.

In the meantime the thing seemed to realize that my bed was empty and was now moving across the room directly into the moonlight. I was now able to see its "face". If you could call it that! The only way I can describe it is to tell you that it looked just like "crumpled linen"! It was quite dreadful! As I stared at that horrible, horrible vision I knew that if my eyes stayed on it for much longer I would go completely mad with fear. Suddenly the creature began to rush around the room in a mad zigzag pattern and as it did the corner of its garment brushed my cheek, causing me to give a cry of terror. This immediately alerted it to my position. In one leap it was on me. Just seconds later it had me by the throat and was bending me backwards over the sill of the open window.

As that awful, crumpled face came within just millimetres of my own I could stand no more. I am ashamed to admit it, but I began to scream and scream and scream.

The door to my bedroom burst open and Colonel Wilson rushed in. He was across the room in a couple of bounds. And just moments later my attacker was gone! All that remained of it was a crumpled heap of bedclothes.

I know that if Colonel Wilson had not come in just then I would have gone completely mad or fallen to my death!

The next morning the Colonel took a small object from my room and threw it as far out to sea as he could. At around the same time the staff made a small bonfire behind the hotel. I think you can guess what the objects of these actions were so I will say no more about them.

Four months on I still do not know what caused this thing to happen to me nor do I wish to give it any more thought. It has quite unhinged me. Even in my own house I am unable to pass a coat hanging on a hook without being seized by terror. The sight of my own bedclothes leaves me trembling with fear. I am terrified that at any moment, it will come back and finish what it started on that awful night! I have tried to get back to being my old self but with little success. Only last week I took a twilight walk in the fields near my house in an attempt to get back to a normal life. I had only been out ten minutes when the sight of a scarecrow standing in a frost-covered field sent me screaming for my front door. Dear, dear colleagues, if anyone ever mentions the word "ghost" to you please do not laugh or mock them. I now know that such horrors do exist. And as a result ... I live in constant fear.

Yours sincerely,

Professor Parkins

The good (and bad) ghost guide

In a way the spook in M R James's story fits lots of people's idea of a typical cartoon or movie ghost. In other words, an over-excitable bed sheet! But the "movie duvet" is only one particular variety of ghost. There are masses more. Here are some spooks that might go "bump" in your night!

Radiant boys

These are the ghosts of boys who've been murdered by their mums. (Why? For having untidy bedrooms of course!) They glow all over and therefore come in really useful during power cuts.

Don't go out of your way to look for radiant boys because if you do meet one it will bring you bad luck! The famous Victorian politician, Lord Castlereagh, once saw one, then had lots of bad luck, including killing himself with his own penknife.

Phone ghosts

These are spooks to send a shiver down your *line*! You hear them but don't see them. Here's a phone-omenally weird story about someone who is said to have spoken to one. A woman hadn't seen her friend for a long time, then one night she had a terrible dream in which she saw this same friend sliding into a pool of blood! She was so alarmed by this that she immediately telephoned her pal to make sure she was OK. The friend answered and said that yes, she was fine, but had actually been in hospital and would be going in again quite soon. When the woman said that she'd pop round and see her, the friend told her not to bother and said she'd phone her back quite soon. The telephone call never came, so after a few days the woman phoned her friend again. This time the phone was answered by a relative who told her that her friend had been dead ... for the last six months! Oooer!

Arrival cases

Arrival cases aren't the ghosts of people who've actually died – they're living ghosts. So *you* too can be an arrival case. Arrival cases result from living people wanting to be in another place so strongly that they actually "project" themselves there in spirit form. And often without knowing it! (So what's the point?) A man had wanted to go to Norway for ages but never quite got round to it. However, after many years he finally got his luggage together and nipped off to the country of his dreams. When he arrived at his hotel the clerk at the reception desk said, "Nice to see *you* back again, sir!" and when he went into a shop the assistant said, "Well I never. We haven't seen *you* for ages!" All this left him wondering whether he'd got a double or whether his soul had been craftily nipping off for little hols of its own without bothering to tell him!

Projecting yourself into another place could obviously come in really handy if you ever fancy a day off school.

But if you're thinking of trying it, please seek the advice of an expert first. This sort of thing takes practice!

Doppelgängers

Doppelgängers are a sort of a ghostly "double". Just like arrival cases, they're living ghosts, but they aren't nearly so fond of travel. Empress Catherine of Russia was said to have had a *doppelgänger*. One day she found it sitting on her throne and became so angry that she immediately ordered her soldiers to shoot it. (Yes, she was "beside herself" with rage!) A man in Chicago saw his *doppelgänger* every time he had a migraine headache. It was fond of sitting opposite him at the table and imitating his every movement!

Warning: If you walk into the bathroom one morning and come face to face with *your* own *doppelgänger* ... *do* *not* be alarmed! You are probably looking into the thing that sensible, less excitable people call "a mirror".

Gremlins

Although you may still occasionally hear someone say that something's not working too well because "it's had an attack of the gremlins", there don't seem to be as many of these ghastly little creatures about as there used to be. They were first seen by World War One aircraft pilots who found them a bit of a nuisance because they did things like biting through operating cables, drinking aircraft fuel and nipping gunners just as they were lining up their sights on an enemy target.

But they also came in incredibly handy if you needed to explain why you'd botched your mission! As the government didn't want reports of gremlins getting out and causing panic amongst the public (who were upset enough as it was) they kept them a secret until 1922.

The next time gremlins cropped up in large numbers was in World War Two, when they sometimes helped pilots fly damaged aeroplanes. The best way to describe them would be as little goblins, but mistier. A pilot who was asked what *his* gremlin looked like said it was six inches tall, a cross between a rabbit and a bull terrier and was wearing suction boots. Hmm! Another one said *his* gremlin was 12 inches tall, humanoid in appearance and was wearing a red ruffled jacket and green britches – obviously on its way to a "fancy gremlin" party. Another pilot said *his* gremlin had webbed feet with a fin on each heel.

Even the famous flyer, Charles Lindbergh, said he saw some gremlins in the cockpit of his plane when he was making his epic flight across the Atlantic in 1927. He said they chatted to him and gave him useful tips. Of course, the fact that he'd had no sleep for over 33 hours would have had no effect on his imagination and judgement whatsoever!

Grey ladies

Grey ladies are ghosts of women who have died violently or just sort of faded away because they couldn't be close to their loved ones. Or couldn't get *away* from their *unloved* ones! Mary Norris Topham was married to Lord Sidney Beauclerk but couldn't stand the sight of him so she jumped in the moat at Speke Hall where they lived. It's said that her ghost still rocks her child's cradle in the tapestry room there.

The family of a girl called Dorothy who lived at Salmesbury Hall in Lancashire were Catholics but Dorothy loved a Protestant. During a secret meeting the lovers made plans to run away together but her brother, who just happened to be hiding in the bushes, overheard them and decided to save his sister from "disgrace". Him and his two mates bumped off Dorothy's fellah and secretly buried his body. Dorothy was sent away to a convent where she died after becoming completely "Dotty". She can now be seen wandering the grounds of Salmesbury with her boyfriend, accompanied by the sounds of crying and wailing and whatnot.

Celebrity ghosts

For some strange reason there seem to be more ghosts of famous people than there are of ordinary bods. Perhaps the "movers and shakers" of the world like to make just as big a noise in death as they did in life? Despite the fact that he's been dead 135 years Abraham Lincoln is forever wandering around the White House and frightening people silly (or silly people, as the case may be). Queen Wilhemina of the Netherlands (an otherwise dignified and sensible royal person) was so upset when he came into her bedroom there one night that she fainted on the spot.

SORRY, MA'AM! WRONG ROOM!

The Tower of London is "groaning" with famous ghosts. The most troublesome one is Margaret, Countess of Salisbury, who's still trying to get over her horrendous execution. Henry VIII ordered that the 70-year-old Maggie be given the chop. Margaret wasn't too keen on losing her head so the axeman ended up chasing her around, making wild swipes at her every time he got within striking distance. And he wasn't exactly helped by the fact that he was wearing a blindfold! (Perhaps he couldn't stand the sight of blood?)

Poltergeists

Despite what some people think, poltergeists are not the ghosts of dead chickens or parrots. They're actually extremely mischievous and destructive spirits who get their kicks from breaking things, throwing things and causing chaos in selected households. Poltergeists are really hard to track and get to grips with because they're completely invisible. Hundreds of ordinary families are said to have been terrorized by poltergeists. Some have even left their homes because they couldn't stand these "hauntings by tauntings" any longer!

Headless ghosts

If you lived in the olden days and you were a) important or b) in the habit of fighting a lot, there was a good chance that at some point during your life you would become separated from your head. As more intelligent readers will realize, this significant life event was usually accompanied by the dramatic and upsetting experience known as death. It was generally thought that someone who'd met their end in this way could never be peaceful until they managed to get back together with their noddle. As a result, history is full of tales of headless ghosts wandering round looking for vanished bonces.

The task of these poor bods was made doubly difficult by the fact that they'd so thoughtlessly left their eyes in the very head they were looking for! Who'd be a headless ghost! It's enough to do your head in, isn't it?

Shrouded ghosts

All right, calm down all you traditionalists and cartoon phantom fans, we'll have the "over-excited bed sheet" variety now! Over the centuries people have sort of got it into their heads that ghosts wander around looking like flying bedspreads because in olden times people used to be buried in a white robe known as a shroud. It was assumed that when they rose from the grave to do their hauntings their ghosts would do the decent thing and keep their shroud on. After all, it would be bad enough to be frightened by an ordinary ghost, but to be frightened by a *completely nude* ghost just doesn't ... *bare* thinking about, does it?

The Body Snatchers

The spooky tale that you're about to read is by Robert
Louis Stevenson (1850–1894), the creator of Dr Jekyll
and Mr Hyde. Robert got the idea for "The Body
Snatchers" (1884) from a real life tale of terror that took
place in Edinburgh in the 1820s. A pair of ghoulish
criminals called Burke and Hare visited graveyards in
the dead of night and dug up freshly buried bodies. If
they couldn't manage to come up with a dead body
they'd go off and find a live one ... and murder it! They
then took the bodies to a Dr Knox and said something
like, "Got a nice one here, mate. Fell off the back of a
hearse! Nudge nudge, wink wink!" Dr Knox would hand
over some dosh, then practise his surgery skills on the
body to his heart's content (or *its* heart's contents!).

You'll be glad to know that Burke and Hare were
finally caught and punished after Hare snitched on his
mate. In Robert's story it's a couple of trainee doctors
who discover that disturbing the dead can lead to
something dead disturbing!

A corpse and robbers story

Years ago I used to pass many a pleasant evening at a Suffolk inn in the company of the landlord, the local undertaker and a retired doctor called Fettes.

One day, a man staying at the inn became ill and his own doctor came up from London to attend him.

"Dr Macfarlane's upstairs, looking after the gentleman what's been taken poorly," said the landlord, as the four of us sat drinking in the bar.

"*What* was that name you just said?" said Fettes, suddenly looking shaken.

"Dr Macfarlane," repeated the landlord, giving Fettes a puzzled stare.

"*Macfarlane?*" gasped Fettes. "Tell me, landlord! What does this Macfarlane *look* like?"

"Silver hair, but not *that* old," said the landlord. "Look, here he comes now!"

At that instant Fettes caught sight of the doctor, turned as white as a sheet, jumped out of his seat and cried, "You, Macfarlane!", barring his way as he did.

This Dr Macfarlane stared at Fettes in disbelief and said, "Fettes ... you!"

"Yes!" said Fettes angrily. "Did you think that *I* was dead too?"

Ignoring the question completely, the doctor tried to push his way to the door but Fettes caught him by the arm and whispered, "Have you seen *it* again?"

At these words Macfarlane let out a yell of terror, put his hands over his head and rushed out into the street. And that was the last we ever saw of him.

Fettes refused to say another word about this strange meeting so we were left completely in the dark, wondering what strange and terrible secret these two medical men shared.

A few months later, I happened to be at Fettes' house when he suddenly said to me, "Do you remember that unfortunate business with Dr Macfarlane? Well, if you could spare me a little of your time I think I am ready to tell you about it now. But please do not breathe a word of it to another soul until I am dead!" Well, Fettes has been gone many a year now. So here is the story he told me...

THE WHOLE THING BEGAN WHEN FETTES WAS A YOUNG MEDICAL STUDENT IN EDINBURGH. HE'D GOT ON WELL AND HAD BEEN GIVEN THE JOB OF ASSISTING THE FAMOUS SURGEON, MR K, AT HIS ANATOMY DEMONSTRATIONS.

NOW, THIS IS LITTLE PIGGIUS. WE REMOVE IT LIKE THIS. MR FETTES, SCALPEL PLEASE.

YES, SIR.

MR K IS AT THE CUTTING EDGE OF MODERN SURGERY.

ONE OF HIS DUTIES WAS TO TAKE DELIVERY OF THE BODIES WHICH MR K USED IN HIS DEMONSTRATIONS AND THE STUDENTS PRACTISED ON. THIS WAS ALWAYS DONE IN THE DEAD OF NIGHT. WHY? BECAUSE THE BODIES WERE PINCHED FROM GRAVEYARDS!

'NOTHER STIFF FOR MR K, GOV'NOR!

DEAD WEIGHT TOO. PHEW ... WHAT A LIFE!

STICK IT OVER THERE, LADS. HOW MUCH DO I OWE YOU?

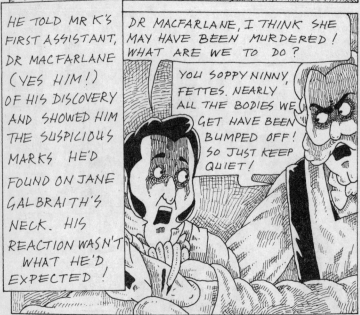

ONE DAY DR MACFARLANE AND FETTES WENT ON A PUB CRAWL WITH A MAN NAMED GREY. HE WAS HORRIBLE BUT HE HAD SOME SORT OF POWER OVER MACFARLANE. (FETTES SUSPECTED THAT HE KNEW ABOUT THE GRAVE-ROBBING SCAM!)

MACFARLANE, BUY ME ANOTHER DRINK ... NOW!

YES, GREY. ALL RIGHT THEN.

SEETHE SEETHE ... GNASH GNASH.

WHAT A RUDE LITTLE MAN! WHY DOES HE ALLOW HIM TO GET AWAY WITH IT?

MACFARLANE! A CORPSE!? BUT HOW DID YOU ...?

YOU'LL SEE! JUST GIVE ME A HAND!

EARLY THE NEXT MORNING, SOMETIME BEFORE DAWN, HE WAS WOKEN BY A KNOCK AT THE FRONT DOOR. IT WAS THE SIGNAL THE GRAVE ROBBERS USED! BUT HE WASN'T EXPECTING THEM! HE OPENED THE DOOR AND FOUND MACFARLANE ON THE STEP. HIS PONY AND TRAP WERE PARKED NEARBY AND HE WAS HOLDING UP A LARGE SACK!

THEY GOT THE SACK UP ON TO THE TABLE. THEN MACFARLANE TOLD FETTES TO LOOK AT THE FACE.

OH NO! IT'S GREY!

YES. HE'LL MAKE A GOOD SPECIMEN. THAT STUDENT RICHARDSON CAN HAVE HIS HEAD. NOW GIVE ME SOME OF MR K'S MONEY FOR THE BODY.

THE NEXT DAY GREY WAS DIVIDED UP AMONGST THE STUDENTS. NOW THEY COULD ALL HAVE A SLICE OF THE ACTION AND FETTES SOON GOT OVER HIS WORRIES. ESPECIALLY WHEN MACFARLANE GAVE HIM SOME OF THE CORPSE MONEY. AND YES, RICHARDSON DID GET THE HEAD!

I PAID AN ARM AND A LEG FOR THESE.

LEND US A HAND, OLD CHAP.

MR K AND THE STUDENTS SOON RAN SHORT OF BODIES AGAIN. SO MACFARLANE AND FETTES WENT TO A QUIET GRAVE-YARD AND STOLE THE BODY OF A FARMER'S WIFE WHO'D BEEN BURIED THE DAY BEFORE.

(PANT PANT GASP). THAT'S IT THEN! WE'LL JUST WHIP OFF THE LID, THEN WE'LL HAVE HER OUT!

WE SHOULD GET A GOOD FEW QUID FOR THIS ONE. HA HA HA!

CLANK CRUNCH GRIND

THEY PROPPED THE SACK CONTAINING THE WOMAN'S BODY BETWEEN THEM. AS THE GIG BOUNCED ALONG THE BODY BUMPED FROM SIDE TO SIDE AS IF IT WERE ALIVE!

AND LISTEN TO THOSE DOGS.

THIS RAIN IS TERRIBLE.

I'VE GOT A VERY BAD FEELING ABOUT THIS ONE.

YES! SO HAVE I. BUT I CAN'T PUT MY FINGER ON IT!

HOWLLLL

HOWLLLL

AS THE SACK GOT WETTER AND WETTER IT MOULDED ITSELF TO THE BODY. THEY BOTH LOOKED AT IT AND INSTANTLY KNEW THAT SOME HORRIBLE CHANGE HAD TAKEN PLACE.

THAT DOESN'T LOOK LIKE A WOMAN'S BODY!

IT WAS A WOMAN WHEN WE PUT HER IN. WE BETTER LIGHT THE LAMP.

AAAAGH! GREY!

MOMENTS AFTER THE LIGHT HAD FALLEN ON THAT FACE THEY KNEW SO WELL, THEY LEAPT FROM THE GIG AND RAN SCREAMING INTO THE NIGHT. THE LAMP CRASHED TO THE ROAD AND THE HORSE GALLOPED OFF IN THE DIRECTION OF EDINBURGH, PULLING THE DEAD AND LONG-DISSECTED GREY!

OOER! IT'S HIM! IT'S 'ORRIBLE!

Spoof spooks and phoney phantoms

That's a great story but some people might find it just a bit far-fetched. Well, it *was* a work of fiction. But what about "real" ghost stories. Just how many of them are finally proved to be "genuine"? About half? Less than that? Or none at all?

OF COURSE NOT!

No one knows for sure, but quite a few reports of so called "hauntings" do turn out to be mistakes. Either that or some mischievous rascal has decided to lead lots of innocent bods on a wild ghost chase! Like these:

The preacher-creature feature
As the mist rose off the river Thames and swirled around the London dockside warehouses of Wapping a strange apparition floated through the gloom. It was a vicar, but not an ordinary vicar – his vicar's outfit was about three hundred years out of date. Why? Because he was a ghost, of course! Lots of people saw him and said things like, "Ooer, what a beast of a priest!" and "This ghost who is clerical has got us hysterical!" News of the creepy curate first came to light in a magazine article but soon everyone was talking about him and memories were being jogged all over the place!

And all the time the fuss was going on, Frank Smythe, the journalist who'd written the feature, was having a right good snicker about the spooky vicar. Because he'd *invented* him! Which just goes to show, "You can *fool* some of the people some of the time ... but if they come from Wapping ... you can *ghoul* them *all* of the time!"

Real ghosts ... seen on the screen at Hallowe'en!
In the early 1990s BBC television showed a documentary called Ghostwatch in which all sorts of weird stuff went on, including sightings of strange lights, equipment inexplicably breaking down mid-broadcast and reporters being so petrified that they shivered in their shoes. The whole spoof (don't say you hadn't realized!) was so convincing that viewers were scared out of their (dim?) wits. Some actually phoned the TV company to say they too were experiencing ghostly phenomena in their own homes as they watched!

Phenomenal Phil – the spook who took over...

In 1971 a bunch of psychic reseachers in Canada tried to get in touch with a spook called Philip. He was the ghost of a long-dead nobleman who'd been a mate of Oliver Cromwell. Phil was married but, being an open-air lover and whatnot, he met up with a beautiful gypsy girl and began going on long nature walks with her. However, they'd hardly got to know each other when the poor girl was chosen by *What Witch* magazine as their hot tip for the month and burned at the stake.

Philip was so cut up about this that he killed himself and soon afterwards began wandering his estate in the shape of a ghost.

After lots and lots of seance-type meetings the researchers actually managed to make contact with Philip in 1973. And the more they talked to him, the more chatty he became, bombarding them with tons of fascinating details about his life and times. The researchers were all absolutely ghoul-smacked by this ... mainly because it was them who'd invented Philip in the first place! Yes, they'd cooked him up to see if ghosts are nothing more than a product of the human subconscious mind! And now he'd "come to life" and was driving them nuts!

At one point one of the boffs became so exasperated with Phil rabbiting on about his life in the seventeenth century and how vegetables really tasted like vegetables in those days and how nowadays you couldn't get a decent set of spurs for love nor money that he yelled, "I've had my Phil of you! Shut your gob ... you great paranormal twit! You *aren't* a ghost! You're a fictitious historical character who we invented in the interest of scientific research!"

At which point Philip got the hump and disappeared for months. It took an awful lot of persuading to get him to return, too! Now, is this weird or isn't it? Fancy inventing a ghost who actually becomes quite "real" in the minds of the group of people who thought him up in the first place! And what does this say about all the thousands of sightings of spooks and the people who reckon they've seen them. Makes you think, doesn't it?

YES, AND I IMAGINE YOU LOT EVERY TIME I DO A HAUNTING!

The Horla

The next slot in our ghastly line-up is filled with "The Horla" (1887) by French writer Guy de Maupassant (1850–93). It's about a man whose very nice life is completely ruined when a mysterious "presence" suddenly turns up and proceeds to make him feel *utterly* miserable and tormented. Fortunately though, he never becomes so miserable that he stops writing his dairy, so we're able to follow his terrible tale to its awful end!

Some people who've read the story have suggested the diary writer is actually imagining the whole thing. They reckon he's putting the blame for feeling down in the dumps on to a non-existent spook. Guy himself was known to be a bit of a misery guts at times and he knew all about the dangers of letting your imagination run away with you. At one point his character actually talks of the way your mind can play tricks on you and invent phantoms to fill the spaces in your life. (What do you fill yours with?) Anyway, you'll have to decide yourself whether the spook's real or not!

Welcome to my world

<u>May 8th</u>

Today has been absolutely brilliant! "Forget work!" I thought to myself as I leapt out of bed. "I need some quality time!" So I spent the whole morning relaxing, just lying on the grass in the front garden. It's absolutely great living in this old house next to the river. There's so much to see! At about eleven o'clock I checked out the most wonderful sight: a whole load of enormous sailing boats being pulled up the Seine ... all by a tiny, tiny tug! The last and best of them was a magnificent three-masted schooner, from Brazil I think. I was so moved by the beautiful sight of this wonderful vessel that I just had to do something. So I jumped up and saluted it. Well, if I'm honest, it was more of a cheery wave than a salute!

<u>May 15th</u>

Have been feeling absolutely terrible for the last seven days!

No idea what's wrong with me. My body has been seized by some sort of fever and I'm as miserable as miserable can be. Added to which, I seem to have the constant feeling that something really terrible is about to happen to me. It's quite dreadful!

May 23rd

Still no better. Probably worse, if I'm honest. Headaches, shivering, sore throat ... and so utterly fed up! I've been to the doctor's and he told me that I'm "a bit run down". He said I should "take plenty of shower baths"! I ask you! What good is that going to do?

Doctor

June 5th

I'm getting worse (if that's possible). My most upsetting moments come during the night. I sleep an hour or two and then I wake, all feverish and anxious! I used to be such a good sleeper too! When I do fall into the half-conscious state that now passes for sleep I get the most horrible feeling that someone is coming to my bedside, looking at me, touching me, climbing on to my bed, kneeling on my chest, taking my neck in their hands and squeezing it... harder and harder, until I cannot breathe! It's more than a feeling actually! It's almost as if I know they're there. If that makes sense? I want to cry out and throw them off! But I can't. I'm paralysed with fear and completely at their mercy! Of course, when I do finally wake I discover that there's no one there. Most disturbing really. Whatever can be happening to me?

=June 9th

In order to tire myself out and try to get a decent night's sleep I've started going for long walks. Yesterday my route took me through the forest. Just as I was passing through the loneliest and deepest part of the woods I suddenly got the feeling that I was no longer alone. It felt as if someone was walking at my heels... close enough to touch me! I stopped and turned. But there wasn't a soul about!

=June 12th

Nothing I do will rid me of my feelings

of unhappiness and fear. I think the only thing left is for me to take a short holiday and hope that it will be the "pick-me-up" I need! I have decided to go to the seaside in Brittany. I leave next week.

= June 22nd

Brittany is perfectly lovely at this time of year. And the sea air is so invigorating! I am definitely feeling better already. Yes, I did need a holiday!

= June 24th

Still in Brittany. Today I have been to the Mont St Michel. What a great sight the Abbey is, standing as it does on that huge rock in the sea. One of the monks kindly showed me around and as we were climbing to the top of the tallest tower he told me an odd story. Apparently, the local people say you can hear strange voices arguing on the sands below the Abbey at night. The fishermen hereabouts say they have seen a mysterious cloaked shepherd down there. He has two goats. One has the face of a woman and the other, a man. They are said to quarrel in human voices for some time, then they begin bleating with all their might. When I asked the monk if he believed the story he gave me a questioning look and said, "We only see a fraction of what goes on on this earth. Take, for example, the wind. Think what awesome power it has! It can blow down buildings, sink ships... and kill people! But it is completely invisible." I think he has a point. This holiday is turning out to be most interesting!

= July 2nd

I am home. And completely cured, I am glad to say! Hurrah! My wonderful holiday has done the trick.

= July 3rd

Not feeling too good today. Slept rather badly last night. And I noticed that Pierre, my handyman, was looking rather pale. He says that he has been feeling bad ever since my holiday. And that it is almost as if someone has cast a "spell" on him!

Pierre

= July 4th

Last night my nightmare came back. As I slept I felt someone leaning over me, his lips on mine, sucking the life out of me... like a leech. When I awoke I felt drained and exhausted. I fear I am ill again!

= July 5th

I put a full jug of water by my bed last night. As usual I was woken by my nightmare. Feeling drained and dry-mouthed I lifted the jug to pour myself a drink. But nothing came. The jug was empty! I do not remember drinking it. So how can this be? Maybe I'm losing my reason?

= July 6th

It happened again! The business with the water jug. I must surely be going mad.

= July 9th

Maybe it is me who is drinking the water? Perhaps I do it in a kind of sleepwalking state that I have no memory of? In which case I am not mad! Tonight I am going to discover the truth. I have put the jug of water near my bed but have wrapped it in a white cloth which I have tied tight with string. Before I go to bed I will rub my lips and my beard and my hands with the very soft lead from an 8B pencil. Then we shall see... once and for all!

= July 10th

Last night I awoke from my nightmare as usual. I got out of bed and went to the table where I had left the water jug. There were no marks on the cloth and the string still held it tightly in place. With my hands trembling like leaves in an autumn breeze I undid the string and removed the cloth. The water had... gone!

= July 12th

I cannot stand it any longer. Perhaps my lonely life in my house by the Seine is not good for me after all? I have an active mind and a vivid imagination. Both are dangerous things if allowed to run riot. Maybe I need the stimulating company of intelligent people around me at all times. It would seem that if left to my own devices I fill the spaces in my head with these phantoms and ridiculous imaginings. Tomorrow I will go to Paris where I will meet my old friends and (hopefully) drive all this nonsense from my mind.

= July 14th

It has been the Bastille Day celebrations here in Paris and I feel like I have been enjoying a second childhood. The bands have been playing, the fireworks exploding and the crowds cheering. All most entertaining! And I have had no bad or fearful thoughts all day. What a relief! I have decided that I definitely ought to get out more! It obviously does me a world of good!

= July 16th =

Something has happened to remind me of the monk's words about not seeing a fraction of what goes on about us. And it has troubled my mind most deeply. Yesterday I went to my cousin's house and met a medical man who has been involved in research about the workings of the human brain. He said that long ago human beings did not have the power to reason and make judgements about the world around them. And as a result, they believed in things like ghosts and spooks and spirits. This doctor then explained that now we have things like language and writing to help us make sense of our world. He predicted that in a few years' time people like him and his colleagues would make incredible discoveries about the mysteries of the human mind. Then he asked my cousin if she would like him to "hypnotize" her and she agreed. As he stared into her eyes she drifted into a deep sleep and I became more and more terrified. When she was completely unconscious he told me to stand behind her, then he took his business card from his wallet and placed it in her hands.

He told her that it was a mirror and that she should look into it and tell him what I was doing as I stood behind her. She stared at the card and, in a slow and peculiar voice that did not sound at all like hers, she said, "He is touching his moustache." And it was true! I was! And then he said, "And now what is he doing?" And she replied, "He is taking a photograph out of his pocket and looking at it." I could hardly believe my ears, for this was exactly what I was doing! "Who is the photograph of?" asked the doctor. "Himself," said my cousin. Now I was doubly astounded. Not only was she right about my actions but there was no way she could have known about that photograph beforehand. I had only had it taken in the hotel a half an hour before! The world we live in is truly one that is cloaked in mystery of all kinds!

= July 22nd

Whilst in Paris I have been going to

dances and parties and have been thoroughly enjoying myself. Maybe it is places that conjure up bad feelings about evil spirits and unknown dreads. I certainly do not feel them while I sit at the Parisian pavement cafés watching all the happy people walk by.

August 2nd

Back home again. Everything fine. Weather lovely. Have been sitting in the garden watching the river flow past. Most relaxing.

August 4th

My servants are quarrelling. For two days now, drinking glasses have been smashed in the cupboards during the night. They blame each other for this. I think I know otherwise. I do not wish to believe it ... but I fear that HE is back.

August 6th

Is HE here or is it just me that is mad? Today I was strolling in my garden admiring my rose bushes when I suddenly saw one of the stalks quite close to me begin to bend as if an invisible hand was clutching it. Next moment the stem snapped and I saw the flower moving through the air.

For some reason this made me feel quite furious. I rushed to seize it but, as I did, it disappeared.

August 7th

Last night he came and drank the water from my jug again.

August 8th

I can feel him quite close to me but I cannot see him. I am quite afraid. I want to escape from my house but cannot. I do not seem to have the energy or will-power to do so. I feel that he has got me in his hold. Just as the hypnotist doctor had my cousin in his power. Yes, an invisible and supernatural being has taken over my life. I am at his mercy. I am quite desperate for help.

August 17th

In an attempt to discover something of the strange forces that have turned my life into a nightmare I have borrowed a book by a famous professor of the supernatural. Last night I sat up reading it until about one o'clock. Eventually I became too tired to continue and went to my bed and fell asleep. About three quarters of an hour later I awoke and looked towards the chair where I had been reading. The book still lay on its arm. As I watched I saw a page lift and fall! Then another. And another! It was as if the finger of an unseen reader was turning them. And that is how I know that he was there! He was sitting in my chair and reading as I had done. I was enraged. Like a wild beast I leapt from my bed and rushed at him, but as I did the chair tipped and the book fell to the floor. Just as if he had fled the room!

August 19th

Now, at last I understand it all! This morning I read of news from the city of Rio de Janeiro in Brazil. An epidemic of madness is raging around part of that country. Hundreds of tortured souls are leaving their houses, saying they cannot stay in them any longer because they are pursued and terrorized by terrible phantom creatures which come in the night and suck the life from them as they sleep and drink the water from their vessels. Yes, creatures exactly like HIM! So now I know! He must have come with the beautiful three-masted schooner from Brazil. The one I so cheerily (and so stupidly) greeted. This Being must have been on board it and I, with one cheery wave, invited him into my life! He is the thing they call the HORLA. I have no choice now. I must kill him.

August 29th

Today I sat at my table, pretending to write, knowing that he would come and prowl round me as he always does. At last, sensing that he was near to me, I rose from my chair in readiness to attack him. I was going to use my hands and teeth to crush him and tear him to pieces! I turned, and directly opposite me was my wardrobe mirror. I looked into it but saw nothing. My own reflection was not there! He had absorbed me completely. Some moments later my reflection slowly began to re-appear in the mirror. That is the sort of terrible power he has over me. How ever will I kill him?

September 5th

I have had a blacksmith make me a metal door and shutters for my room. They are now in place. The trap is set.

SEPTEMBER 10TH

LAST NIGHT I LEFT MY FRONT DOOR WIDE OPEN AND WAITED FOR HIM TO COME. SUDDENLY I KNEW HE WAS THERE IN MY ROOM WITH ME SO I QUICKLY SLAMMED AND BOLTED THE METAL DOOR AND SHUTTERS. NOW I WAS FRIGHTENED. BUT I COULD SENSE THAT HE WAS ALSO AFRAID! I EDGED TOWARDS THE DOOR AND STOOD WITH MY BACK TIGHT AGAINST IT. I OPENED IT A SPACE, SLID OUT, THEN BOLTED IT BEHIND ME! NOW I HAD HIM!

I RAN DOWN THE STAIRS TO MY SITTING ROOM WHICH IS DIRECTLY BENEATH MY BEDROOM. AS QUICKLY AS I COULD, I POURED THE OIL FROM TWO LARGE LAMPS ALL OVER MY CARPETS AND FURNITURE, THEN DROPPED A LIGHTED MATCH INTO IT! AS FLAMES LICKED GREEDILY AT THE CURTAINS I RACED OUT OF THE HOUSE, DOUBLE-PADLOCKED MY BIG FRONT DOOR, THEN RAN DOWN THE GARDEN AND HID BEHIND A BUSH.

AS I CROUCHED AND WATCHED, THE BIRDS AROUND ME WOKE AND BEGAN TO SCREECH, AND IN THE DISTANCE, DOGS BEGAN TO HOWL. SUDDENLY THE INSIDE OF MY HOUSE WAS LIT UP BY A HUGE WALL OF FLAME! SOON THE

DOWNSTAIRS WINDOWS WERE EXPLODING AND THE WHOLE GROUND FLOOR HAD BECOME A BLAZING INFERNO. AND THEN A HORRENDOUS SHRILL CRY RANG THROUGH THE STILL NIGHT AIR AND TURNED MY BLOOD TO ICE. THE VERY NEXT MOMENT I SAW A WOMAN'S FACE APPEAR AT THE ATTIC WINDOW. AND THEN ANOTHER AT THE NEXT ONE. AND THEN I SAW MY FAITHFUL HANDYMAN AT HIS OWN WINDOW, FRANTICALLY CLAWING AT THE GLASS AND MOUTHING SILENT SCREAMS. I HAD FORGOTTEN THE SERVANTS! IN MY BLIND PANIC TO DESTROY HIM I HAD NOT GIVEN THEM A SINGLE THOUGHT! AND NOW THEY WERE BEING BURNED ALIVE! I LEAPT FROM MY HIDING PLACE AND RAN TOWARDS THE VILLAGE SCREAMING, "FIRE FIRE FIRE!" WHEN I HAD GONE SOME DISTANCE I STOPPED AND TURNED, JUST IN TIME TO SEE THE ROOF OF MY HOUSE CRASH IN! I THOUGHT TO MYSELF, "HE, THE HORLA, IS IN THERE, AND HE IS DEAD!" BUT NOW I'M THINKING, "IS HE DEAD?" AND I'M NOT SO SURE. WOULD A FIRE HAVE KILLED A BODY THAT, UNLIKE OURS, IS INVISIBLE? AND POSSIBLY INDESTRUCTIBLE? PERHAPS HE CAN DIE EVERY DAY AND EXIST AGAIN THE NEXT

NO, I THINK THAT HE IS NOT DEAD. SO NOW THERE IS ONLY ONE THING FOR IT. IF HE, THE HORLA, WILL NOT PERISH... THEN IT IS I... WHO MUST DIE

Global ghosts

So, what do you reckon? Was the Horla real, or not? Brazil, where it's supposed to have come from, is said to be the most haunted country on earth. That's not to say there aren't masses of ghosts in all the other ones. Before you decide where you're going for your next foreign hol', take a butcher's at this lot!

The afrit

An afrit is an Arab ghost and is the demon spirit of a murdered man. It rises up like smoke from the victim's blood, then falls back to the ground and goes around trying to get revenge on whoever did the murder. The only way to stop its horrible malarkey is to drive a new nail into bloodstained ground where the man was done in. But whatever you do ... try not to be afrit of it! (Arf, arf.)

The ankou

An ankou is the ghost of the last person to die in a village at the end of the year. Watch out for them if you ever go on your hols to Britanny in France 'cos that's where most of them hang out. The ankou is very tall and haggard looking (due to being a bit off its food) and can see all around itself. To help it do this it's got a head that revolves 360 degrees (yes, just like a teacher's). The ankou pushes a creaky old hand cart and wanders around wailing and looking for places where someone is about to die. It's got two ghost helpers because in the olden days Breton people were always popping their sabots (French clogs) all over the place and at times things could get a bit hectic.

Tip: If a door-to-door soulsman comes to your house and asks if you've got any old spirits it can have, just firmly say "Not to die ... ankou!" and shut the door in its face!

The ba

A ba is an Egyptian ghost. Unlike other ghosts, the souls of Egyptian corpses generally like to stay in their tombs, but when they do feel like getting a bit of fresh air and exercise they're quite fond of going for a wander around the graveyard. This may well be because the really nice goddess who lives in the tree in the graveyard always

gives them nice cakes and stuff to eat whenever she sees them. If you want to see lots of bas look up in the sky on a cloudless night. There are loads of them up there, all individually illuminated by their own personal oil lamps. Well, this is what the ancient Egyptians believed, but modern people prefer to call them stars. Shout insults at them if you wish – but only if you're brave enough to say *ba to a ghost*.

The bhut

Bhuts are Indian ghosts. They're the spirits of men who have died by execution, accident or suicide. If you meet one you'll recognize it by the fact that it hasn't got a shadow and speaks with a nasal twang – that means it sounds like it's got a clothes peg on its nose. Bhuts can

never rest on earth so you'll never see one lying down. They have poisonous spit and often go round with a big pack of ghost dogs. They're so horrible that if you see one you'll more likely than not die of fright! If you do manage to survive coming face to face with one

you'll get loads of goodies! The only thing they're frightened of is the spice known as turmeric. So watch out for 'I hate spice" ghouls! And talking of ghouls...

The ghoul

This is a word that is used for ghosts in general nowadays but it was originally a type of Middle Eastern demon spirit that feeds on the flesh of humans,

especially the children of nomadic people and corpses stolen from graves. Ghouls live in lonely places like ruined buildings, graveyards and the desert. There are quite a few different types of ghouls but one of the scariest sorts looks just like a normal living woman.

These lady ghouls marry (short-sighted?) men who only find out what they've let themselves in for just after their new bride has told them they look sweet enough to eat!

Keres

Keres are ancient Greek ghosts. The ancient Greeks used to preserve dead bodies in big jars – rather like pickled onions (but not quite so tasty). Sometimes souls would escape from the jars then go around being a right nuisance to the living in the shape of keres. In order to stop keres coming into their houses and annoying them, people painted their door-frames with wet tar so the  keres would stick to them and not be able to come inside. Obviously, if there just happened to have been a mass breakout of keres, everyone's door-frames would be covered with dozens of the things – and end up looking like sticky fly paper on a hot summer's afternoon!

The ch'iang schich

This is a Chinese ghost with problem breath. Or to put it another way, you *die* if it breathes on you! A man and his three pals were looking for somewhere to stay but the inn was full. However, the helpful landlord said they could stay in his barn. As his three mates lay snoring the man heard a noise and saw a "thing" coming towards them. It was the landlord's daughter. The jolly inn-keeper had sort of forgotten to tell the travellers they'd be sharing with her. He'd also forgotten to mention that she was dead! Now, to make matters worse, she'd gone and turned into a ch'iang shich. The horrible creature  gave a quick blast of fatal fumes to the three sleeping beauties and that was the end of them. Next she turned to the man who did the only thing he could. No, of course he didn't offer her an extra strong mint! He held his own breath, jumped out of bed and ran off with old Bacteria Breath in hot pursuit. Eventually it caught up with him and trapped him against a tree. He was so frightened that he fainted as it struck at him with its huge claws. When he awoke at dawn he looked up to see it stuck to the tree by its claws and dead as a doughnut! The man became a lifelong customer of Holiday Inns from that day on.

Lemures

These are ancient Roman ghosts of people who died with no surviving family. They're also *evil* ancient Roman ghosts *and* ancient Roman ghosts of murder victims. To stop lemures popping up out of their tombs the ancient Romans burned black beans around their graves but if they did manage to escape they got rid of them by banging drums and having a three-day-

long festival of *appeasement*. That means a festival to calm them down a bit. During the festival the head of household would get up in the middle of the night, wash their hands three times, put some black beans in their mouth then walk around chanting and throwing beans over their shoulder. In that case shouldn't it have been called the festival of a*beans*ment?

The rolang

This Tibetan spook's absolutely *delightful*. This is how one's made (or not, as the case may be!). A Tibetan sorcerer goes into a dark room with a dead body. He lies on top of it and gives it mouth to mouth resuscitation, like a life guard at the swimming baths, but for slightly more selfish reasons. While the sorcerer's busy snogging the stiff he repeats a magic chant, but only in his head – aloud would be a bit tricky, under the circumstances. After a while the corpse starts to come back to life and begins to thrash around a bit. This is where things can get extremely difficult so the sorcerer has to hang on like, er ... grim death! All of a sudden, the corpse sticks out its tongue and in turn, quick as a flash, the sorcerer bites it off. And that's that – job done! Feeling as chuffed as anything, the sorcerer sticks the tongue in his  pocket, takes it home, dries it, then uses it as an extremely lucky charm (or handy book mark) leaving the poor old corpse completely lost for words. That's the theory! That's what's *supposed* to happen! *However*, if the sorcerer hasn't got staying power and loses control of the corpse during the "snog-in" things turn out rather differently. The corpse goes completely bananas, throws the sorcerer off, kills him, then leaps to its feet and becomes a "rolang" – which, in Tibetan, means "standing corpse". The berserk rolang then goes charging around the local countryside spooking people and causing chaos in general: knocking on doors and running away, letting down bicycle tyres, biting the heads off peasants ... that sort of thing.

The rusalki

You'll be relieved to know that these are nice ghosts. They're the spirits of maidens who've drowned in the rivers of southern Russia.  They're usually beautiful and they live on river islands and help the poor, hard-working, local fishing folk. If you're alert you may see them bathing in the river (now wearing their new water wings, of course) then wringing out their long green hair into the meadow grass at the water's edge. Every so often the fisher folk have festivals where they dance and throw flower garlands to the rusalki.

The Screaming Skull

Quite a few ghosts are said to be ghosts because they aren't happy. Either because a) they died a sudden, unexpected and painful death b) they didn't get the after-death send off (or fancy funeral) they were expecting or c) they're very, very angry with someone and are out to get revenge on them, especially if they're the person, or persons, who were responsible for causing their death in the first place! The next ghost you're going to read about fits all three of these descriptions. It's the subject of a story by F Marion Crawford (1854–1909) called "The Screaming Skull" (1911). It just doesn't seem to want to settle down to a quiet and peaceful after-life. No matter what's done with it! So pull your chair a bit closer to the fire and settle down to this tale of teeth and terror.

Heads you lose

The story I'm going to tell you concerns an old shipmate of mine called Captain Braddock. Just over three months ago he invited me to stay the night at his little cottage which is about a quarter of a mile outside the seaside village of Tredcombe. The Captain's strange tale began to unfold as we sat in front of a blazing fire in his little parlour on that wild and stormy night. A wild and stormy night that I'll *never* forget.

"Smashin' little place you've got here," I said. "Handy for the beach *and* the pub."

"Yes," he said. "My cousin, Dr Luke Pratt, left it to me. He died just before I retired. So I suppose you could say I struck lucky. Which is more than I can say for him."

"What happened to him?" I said.

"I'd prefer not to say," said Captain Braddock. "Him and Mrs Pratt lived here for years but then things sort of ... changed."

"And Mrs Pratt," I said. "Where's she?"

"Dead too," said the Captain. "She died some time before Luke." As he said this a shadow passed over his face, then he added. "It always gives me a bad feeling when I think about Mrs Pratt dying."

"Why's that then?" I said.

At first the Captain seemed reluctant to say any more but then he said, "Oh, I suppose I can tell *you*. You being an old shipmate and that.  Thing is, I feel very *guilty* about her death. You see, just before she passed on, I'd been telling Luke about some Irish lass killing her husbands by drugging them then pouring boiling lead in their ears. When I talked about this Luke seemed to sit up and take notice but I thought no more of it. Then a couple of weeks later I heard that Mrs Pratt had died in her sleep. I remembered how her and Luke were always falling out and how Luke had often treated her bad and ever since then the whole thing's played on my mind."

"Just a coincidence?" I suggested.

"And then there was Bumble," said the Captain, as if he'd not heard me.

"Bumble?" I said.

"Yes, their dog," he continued. "Mrs Pratt adored him but Luke felt different. He said the dog kept staring at him. When Bumble died he as good as told me it was him that put him to sleep. And this wasn't that long after Mrs Pratt's death. Can you see what I'm driving at? I suppose when I found the ladle it made up my mind."

"The ladle?" I said.

"Yes," he said. "When I moved in I was having a big clear out of all their stuff when I found this ladle. It had traces of lead in it."

"Oh, yes," I said. "Now I *can* see what you're getting at!"

"I found something else during that clear out," said the Captain. "It was in one of Mrs Pratt's old hatboxes in the bedroom cupboard."

"What was it?" I said.

"A human skull," said the Captain. "You look surprised. Well, so was I at first, but then, when I thought about it, I decided it was probably normal for a doctor to have a skull lying around. Because of his job. Just as seafarers like you and me have charts in our cabin because of *our* job. So I just left it in the cupboard. Thing is, though, after a while it proved to be a bit of a nuisance."

"In what way?" I said.

"Well, not long after I found it I began to hear noises coming from the bedroom as I sat by the fire of an evening. Sort of rattling, muttering sounds. Like someone having a muffled telephone conversation! Can you believe that? At first I thought it was the wind whistling through the wall so I blocked up all the gaps. But it made no difference! The noises came just the same. And after about a week or so they began to get on my nerves. I decided the only place they possibly *could* be coming from was the hatbox with the skull in it. So I went straight up to the bedroom, opened up the cupboard, grabbed the box and threw it out of the window as far as I could! But listen to this, old friend! Just then the strangest thing happened! At the very moment it was in mid-air, about halfway across the lane out there, the thing began ... *screaming*! And I'm not joking, shipmate. It was ear splitting. Like the noise a big shell makes after it's fired from a cannon! My hair stood on end!"

As the Captain said this I felt the hairs on the nape of my *own* neck prickle and my skin tingle. I don't why, but I just *knew* that he was telling me the truth.

"But that's not all!" he continued. "On no! Not by a long chalk. I hardly slept a wink that night, thinking about that box and that terrible screaming. And it must have been around dawn when I finally dozed off. But only for a few minutes. Because all of a sudden I was woken by this loud knocking on the front door. I looked out of the bedroom window but couldn't see who it was because of the porch roof. Then the knocking started again so I went down and opened up. As I stepped out I felt something bang against my foot. I looked down. There was the skull on the doorstep. It was sort of looking up at me. Like it was expecting me to *pick it up*! Does that sound crazy to you?"

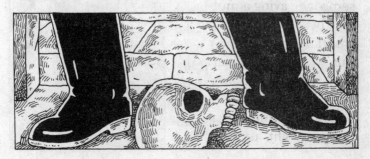

"It's hard to say!" I said. "But tell me! What *did* you do?"

"I did just that. Picked it up, put it in its box which I found on the other side of the lane, then took it back up to the cupboard. And that's where it is now. The only time it's been out of there is when ... ah! There it goes now! Do you hear it?" Captain Braddock stopped and pointed to the ceiling, signalling for me to listen.

And he was right. Despite the gale which was howling around the cottage and getting stronger by the moment, I *did* hear something. It was a sort of muffled, chattering sound, followed by what sounded like high-pitched sobbing. "Are you sure that's it?" I said, beginning to feel more than a little nervous. "Oh yes ... definitely!" he replied. "There's no mistaking it! It always starts up like that when I'm talking about it. Now, where was I? Yes, the only time it's been out since is when Trehearn found the jaw."

"The jaw?" I said.

"That's right," said the Captain. "Oh, I forgot to tell you, didn't I? When I first found the thing it had no lower jaw. Then one day, old Trehearn, who does the garden for me, was digging a celery trench when he found a human jawbone. Being curious I thought I'd try it on the skull. And it fitted perfect! *Now*, listen to this! Just as I was fitting it ... the teeth closed shut on my fingers. Snap! Like that! I suppose I *could* have been imagining it, but it really did feel like it bit me. Ah there it goes again!"

This time there was no mistaking it. A series of ear-splitting yowls and screeches had broken out directly above us. Like someone would make if they were very, very angry. Or in pain. In spite of the blazing fire I felt a chill creep over my whole body and began to wish that I was as far away from those awful sounds as possible.

"Old Trehearn's for taking the thing to the grave-yard," went on the Captain, ignoring the horrendous screaming that was now echoing around the upper floor of the cottage.

"He says we should bury it once and for all and be done with it. But somehow I can't bring myself to. I feel it belongs in this house. After all it was *her* home, wasn't it?" It surprised me when he said this, but thinking back, I don't suppose I should have been. After all, everything sort of pointed to what he was hinting at.

"You mean to say you think that the skull is that of Mrs...?"

"Well what do *you* think?" said the Captain. "Now! I tell you what. I'll fetch it down for you so you can take a look at it. All right?"

In all honesty, I'd sooner have sailed five times around the Horn in a leaky tramp steamer than see that awful thing on that terrible night. But Captain Braddock *was* my old shipmate of thirty years and more. And I think he *needed* to show it to me. For his own peace of mind. So I just nodded and quietly said, "Yes, why not?" He took a candle and started upstairs but had only gone a couple of steps when the gale suddenly increased tenfold in its ferocity. There was the most almighty crash and all at once the little window of the front parlour burst open, making the curtains twist and flap like a pair of banshees and the fire roar like a mad thing.

"Would you look at *that*!" cried the Captain with a fearful look. "*That's* never happened before! Look, be a good fellow and shut the thing for me. While I go up and get the box!"

By the time he returned I'd managed to get the window shut, but not without a struggle. As he placed the box on the table in front of us the screams became even louder and wilder. But now they didn't seem to be coming from up above, like before. They now seemed to be coming from *outside* the cottage!

"Listen!" said Captain Braddock, as he fumbled with the box lid. "Those screams *aren't* coming from in here, are they? So *maybe* I've been wrong all along. Maybe it *is* something else that's making them. I've always had the feeling that might be the case! Anyway, here goes, you can see the thing for yourself. See what you think!" He took the lid off the box. It was empty!

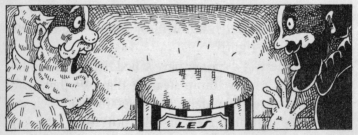

He looked as shocked and terrified as *I* felt. "It must have been Trehearn!" he said quickly, obviously trying to control his rising panic. "It's *got* to be! How else could it have got out? He *must* have taken it. Probably to the graveyard to bury it. So it'll lie quiet ... once and for ever!"

As the Captain spoke these words, he turned the box over and we heard a dull thud as something heavy hit the floor. He dropped to his hands and knees, scrabbled around a bit, then held something out to me. It was a small lump of lead.

"This is it!" he said. "I've felt it rattle about inside the skull before. But I didn't like to think of it. It's definitely what did for her though! Oh, when I think of the *agony* she must have gone through! Having boiling lead poured in her brain like that. That poor little woman. And it was all *my* fault you know! She wouldn't even have had time to scream! And now she screams at me because she *hates* me! She hates me you know! She really does!"

On that last word, as if to prove him right, the night air outside the cottage was suddenly filled with yet another volley of blood-curdling screams, each one louder and more terrifying than the last.

"It's out there! It's out there!" cried the Captain, gripping my arm so hard it hurt, his face the colour of ash. "We've just *got* to find it. It's *never* been this bad before. Ever! Will you *please, please* help me?"

I think at that moment Captain Braddock was probably half insane with fear. And me not far off, if truth be told! Trying to ignore the quaking of my knees and the deafening thump of my own bursting heart, I gathered up my courage and said, "Yes, of course I will. But if we do find it, don't you think we ought to bury it?"

"Yes, yes!" he sobbed. "*Anything*! *Anything* you say! I'll get a lantern and a shovel!"

The gale almost blew us off our feet as we staggered around the cottage in the pitch darkness, desperately casting the light of the flickering lantern this way and that.

But, try as we might, we couldn't find the thing. We certainly heard it though. Those screams were almost constant now! After ten minutes of fruitless searching we paused, trying to think of what to do next. And that's when we heard the knocking.

"It's there! It's there!" yelled the Captain. "Listen! It wants to get back in! Look, we shut the door! Quick! Open the door, man! Open the door! Let it back in!"

Without thinking, I ran to the door, lifted the latch and almost fell into the cottage. A moment later I *saw* the loathsome thing for the first time! It was rolling across the kitchen floor. Towards *me*! Quite slowly, deliberately and purposefully. Almost as if it *knew* I was there! I screamed and leapt back in terror, completely horrified and appalled.

"Stand still! It's nothing!" yelled Captain Braddock. "It's just the wind blowing it. Be still, man! Be still!"

But I didn't believe him. And I don't think he believed himself.

"Grab it!" he bellowed, rushing towards me with the hatbox. "Grab it, man! Now!" And unthinkingly, I obeyed his orders. Just as I'd done aboard ship a thousand times before. As I made contact with the cold, cold bone I felt pressure on my fingers and a searing pain shoot up my arm. I looked at my hand. The awful thing's jaws had clamped shut on it! I screamed again, raised my arm and shook it for all I was worth.

Then, with relief, I watched the dreadful object fall into the waiting box. Without another word, the Captain slammed down the lid and raced upstairs with his horrendous package, leaving me to nurse my bloodied fingers. He returned a few minutes later, looking slightly calmer.

"I've locked it in the cupboard," he gasped. "It should be quieter now. It sometimes does that you know. Goes sort of crazy, then calms down for the night. I think we'd better have another drink."

With all thoughts of burying the skull forgotten, we slumped in our armchairs by the fire, sipping our whiskies, both lost in thought as we reflected on the awful events of the evening. After about twenty minutes or so, I finally roused myself and said, "Look Captain Braddock, there's one thing I've just got to know. Remember how you said that your cousin, Dr Luke Pratt, had died sometime before you came here. Will you tell me what *did* happen to him?"

The Captain paused for a moment, then said, "All right, I suppose I might as well tell you. You'll only hear it from elsewhere sooner or later, anyway." He paused again, sighed, took a large sip of his whiskey, then said, "Dr Luke was found dead on the beach by one of the local fisherman. When the authorities examined his body they found marks all over his throat. But he'd not been robbed or anything. The verdict they put down on his death certificate was that he'd come to his end, '*By the hands or teeth of some person or animal unknown*'.

Some of the jury thought that he'd perhaps been thrown down by a big dog that had gripped his windpipe with its teeth. But none of them could be sure. And they had no idea why he'd gone there. Not far from him, and quite near the water's edge, they found the hatbox. And right next to his head lay...

"The skull?" I said.

"Yes, that's right," he said.

That was the last time I ever saw Captain Braddock. The following morning I set off for my ship at Portsmouth long before my old friend was out of his bed. I left him a "thank you" note on the kitchen table saying I hoped to see him again quite shortly. A few weeks after this, on returning from a short voyage to the Azores, I happened to dock at Plymouth again, where I bought a copy of the local newspaper. As I flipped through it I saw an article that made my blood run cold. I've attached the clipping so you can read it for yourself. Maybe when you've done so you'll be able to come to your own conclusions ... just as I've come to mine.

SOUTH WESTERN MERCURY

November 1906

STRANGE DEATH OF RETIRED SEA CAPTAIN

The people of the tiny fishing village of Tredcombe are feeling utterly horrified and alarmed by the mysterious death of Captain Charles Braddock. Captain Braddock was found dead in his bed last Tuesday morning. On examination of his body it was discovered that his throat had been viciously bitten by a human attacker. The attack had taken place with such force and ferocity that Captain Braddock's windpipe had been crushed, thus causing his death. It is not known how the murderer could have entered his house as there was no sign of a forced entry.

A police alert has been put out that a dangerous maniac is on the loose in the area. A surgeon who examined the wounds is of the opinion that Captain Braddock's killer is a woman because of the small size of jaw indicated by the bite marks.

CAPTAIN BRADDOCK GOT IT IN THE NECK!!

The local coroner has come to the conclusion that Captain Braddock died "by the hands or teeth of some person or animal unknown". Captain Braddock was a widower who lived alone. He leaves no children.

Ghost-hunting guide for brave spirits

If you're more the "up-and-at-'em" type, rather than the "cowering-in-a-corner-waiting-for-the-ghost-to-come and-get-you" type, why not get your retaliation in first by going and finding your ghost? To help you get started here's a list of the kit you'll need:

A thermograph

This gadget records changes in temperature on graph paper. If you see the thermograph indicating a sudden drop in temperature you'll know that either **a)** a ghost is close by (they're said to cause "cold spots" wherever they haunt) or **b)** it's time to put on your woolly combinations and drink your hot chocolate. (Do not attempt these two activities at the same time.)

Felt overshoes

These stylish items of soft footwear are worn by all the top ghost-hunters. They **a)** prevent the ghosts from hearing you as you sneak about trying to detect their presence or **b)** make you look so completely stupid that any ghost seeing you will immediately burst out laughing and therefore give away their location.

A torch and some candles

You will no doubt be conducting your hunt in a darkened building (there's no point in doing it with the lights on, it's no fun) so you *will* need some form of illumination.

Really useful tip: Some ghost-hunters stand their candles in jam jars to stop them being blown out by mysterious draughts. (You'll probably find this works much better if you take the jam out of the jar first.)

A house plan or map

You may not be entirely familiar with the place you are investigating. It could have a maze of rooms and corridors in which you might get hopelessly lost (maybe for ever). So carry a house plan or map with you at all times. (You

will probably find it *extra* useful if it's a house plan or map of the place that you're actually investigating.)

Flour, sand and sugar

These will come in incredibly handy ... although they could get you into a sticky situation!

Spread them all over the floor of the place you are exploring. If you return to find footprints, it will be an indication that there is another "presence" in the house – unless of course they are *your* footprints ... in which case, watch where you're treading, big feet!

A notebook

Listen! You may be coming face to face with a real *real* ghost! During moments of high excitement and drama it is easy to get the facts jumbled up in your head or even forget what you have witnessed. With a notebook you will be able to record events as they happen.

Or, having waited absolutely months and not seen a thing, you may want to write yourself a reminder.

An increase in pocket money

You'll need this to pay the wages of your assistants and for the mountain of "high-tech" ghost-hunting gear you'll need to have with you. This will include your thermograph (which you already know about) and possibly **a)** a mobile phone to keep in touch with your team – and to order take-out pizzas **b)** a really "flashy" camera for taking pictures in the dark **c)** a camcorder and tape recorder for evidence – or in case the ghost is in "show-off" mode and feels like doing its well known rendition of favourites from *The Phantom of The Opera* and **d)** a microwave oven to reheat the take-out pizzas after the ghost's cold spot has cooled them down.

Some sticky tape

Ghost-hunters use this to seal up rooms and make sure that intruders can't sneak in and tamper with their detection devices when they nip to the bathroom. Shy ghost hunters also use it seal up the bathroom.

A lot of patience

Ghost-hunting can be a tedious business. Maybe you should take something along to pass the time too. Like a good book!

A pocket full of stones

If you've been hanging around a "haunted" house for absolutely yonks and *still* haven't found a ghost you could always do what ghost-buster Harry Price did. *Cheat!* Ghost-hunting's quite a popular pastime nowadays but Harry was one of its pioneers. During the 1930s he spent lots of time and money checking out Borley Rectory, the so-called "most haunted house in England". He later wrote a book about it all which made him quite famous. However, some years later a reporter described how he'd been with Harry at Borley Rectory when stones had mysteriously begun to fly through the air. He was so frightened by this that he grabbed hold of Harry and discovered that the spook seeker's pockets were full of pebbles!

Another journalist said that Harry had published a photograph of a flying brick as evidence that a poltergeist was at work. It was actually a builder that was at work. He was busy knocking down a wall and merrily lobbing bricks all over the place. Harry had photographed the brick just after he'd thrown it.

The Benadanti – the spook-smashers

If you'd lived in the old days and wanted to be a ghost-buster you'd probably consider yourself lucky if you were born a Benadanti. These old-fashioned seventeenth-century Italian spook-duffer-uppers were people who were born with a thing called a caul. This is a sort of flap of thin skin on top of the head which all babies have when they're in the womb but most people lose before birth. A bit like an organic anorak hood!

The Benadanti kept theirs as a souvenir after it dropped off and wore it around their neck. Having this unusual neck-caul-ace gave them the ability to see ghosts when other people couldn't. So! If you ever go to Italy and see a really old person wearing what looks like an extremely shrivelled leather flying helmet around their neck, who is staring into space, pointing at nothing in particular and gibbering incoherently, they're probably a Benadanti checking out a ghost (or just plain bonkers).

In olden times the Benadanti did a really important job. When the season changed at autumn or spring, they left their own bodies, disguised themselves as animals, and went off and had mass scraps with ghosts and witches who were also in animal disguises. The Benadanti armed themselves with sticks of fennel (trendy celery) while the witches and ghosts were tooled up with blades – which sounds incredibly unfair ... until you realize they were blades of grass!

The Benadanti and witches and ghosts would all meet up in the fields, then do their best to knock the spaghetti out of each other. If the Benadanti won the battle with the spooks the local crops would be good that season but if they lost it was a case of ... "Si, Carlo, thassa right! We gotta mud macaroni for tea, *again!*"

The punch-ups took place at night and if the Benadanti weren't back inside their bodies by cock crow (old-fashioned breakfast TV), boy, were they in *deep* trouble! Try as they might to nip back in through a handy earhole, nostril or back entrance (mmmph! snigger snigger) ... no way could they get back inside themselves! Imagine it! Locked out of your own body! And not just for twenty-four hours! The poor Benadanti were condemned to wander the earth until their bodies were ready to die. Confused? Well, so were the Benadanti!

The Bowmen

The next tinglesome tale is by Arthur Machen (1863–1947) and it involves not just one ghost, but hundreds, maybe even *thousands* of them. But don't run away! Not all ghosts are necessarily nasty! You may even find that you are pleasantly *relieved* when you finally meet this lot. The story's set in the early days of the First World War when the massive and powerful German army was storming across northern France and making short work of anyone who dared oppose it. Things were looking very, very bad for the French, and for the British soldiers (known as "Tommies") who were helping them defend their country. Arthur's story is about the strange experiences of a company of Tommies who were completely outnumbered by the attacking Germans.

When the tale was actually published it caused a right kerfuffle in England, not to mention lots of problems for Arthur. But more of *that* later! Let's take a look at the newspapers of the day to find out just how badly things were going for those brave chaps in the trenches!

THE BUGLE

20TH AUGUST 1914

GRIM NEWS FROM THE FRONT

The first weeks of the war in Europe are turning into a disaster for us and our French allies. Hundreds of thousands of German troops have poured across Belgium and into France. And despite putting up a brave fight the French army has failed to hold its ground. Eighty thousand French troops are now retreating from the oncoming German hordes. A small group of British soldiers are doing their best to give support to the fleeing French but they too are under terrible pressure. What happens in the next few days could affect all of our lives! We will keep you informed. God save the King!

THE BUGLE

21ST AUGUST 1914

EVEN GRIMMER NEWS FROM THE FRONT

I would like to be able to bring you some good news. But I can't! As I write just one thousand brave English lads are giving everything they've got to the hold off three hundred thousand German soldiers! Outnumbered by at least one hundred to one, our plucky boys are defending a small and vitally important corner of northern France.

"Mystic Maud"

Seances a speciality!
Let her bring you news
from the other side!

When I spoke to a top army general in London this morning he told me, "Those lads out there have just got to hang on! They're our last hope. If they don't manage to stop the Germans overrunning that spot it could mean total defeat for all the British and French armies. And I mean total! If that happens there is no telling what will come next! We could be hearing the tramp of German army boots in the towns and villages of England by Christmas!"

All London is overcome by a mood of gloom and doom.

THE BUGLE

22ND AUGUST 1914

GRIMMEST NEWS YET FROM THE FRONT

From our correspondent at the trenches

Oh drat! Can it get any worse? Of the original one thousand brave young British Tommies here, only five hundred remain. The rest have been torn to pieces by German shells. Yesterday I stood side by side with our heroes in the trenches. We were up to our bloomin' necks in muck and bullets. But would you believe it? These heroes still joke about the shells that whistle overhead then mangle them and their comrades to minced meat. They even give them nicknames! These boys don't deserve to die. I will pray for them. I know you will too!

THE BUGLE

24TH AUGUST 1914

FANTASTIC NEWS FROM THE FRONT!

They've done it! Those plucky lads of ours have saved the day. Yesterday, after the huge German cannons had pounded our remaining big guns to scrap metal, wave after wave of German infantry began to advance on the surviving British Tommies. It looked like the end was near. Then suddenly the tide turned! The advancing German troops started to fall like nine pins! Within minutes the battlefield was strewn with enemy dead. Moments later I saw the German advance start to falter. And then they began to retreat. At that moment I knew the day was ours! It is nothing less than a miracle! Hurrah for our boys! Ha ha ha! Take that, Fritz!

THE BERLIN TIMES

24TH AUGUST 1914

DONNER UND BLITZEN!!

Our glorious advance across France has been temporarily halted by a handful of British Tommies. Just when we thought victory was ours, our troops began to go down like skittles! Ten thousand of them were killed!

Afterwards when the bodies were examined it was found that many of them had no wounds on them ... at all! It is all very puzzling – even for us extremely clever Germans! Some people are now saying that those infernal Britishers must have used a newfangled weapon. Maybe shells filled with some special sort of poisonous gas. But I say this is all a load off Tommy-rot! (Hahaha, who says us Germans haff no sense of humour!) Long live the Kaiser!

THE SUNDAY INVESTIGATOR

19TH SEPTEMBER 1914

VICTORY! BY GEORGE?

Did our boys get some heavenly help?

Special Feature by Don Delve
As you all know by now a group of our soldiers in France have pulled off the most amazing victory. The tea rooms and pubs of old England have been abuzz with talk of nothing else for days. All sorts of rumours and explanations have been flying around as to what actually happened. I personally do not question the bravery of our boys for one moment but for them to have overcome the enemy against such overwhelming odds seems almost unbelievable. Even the military experts are secretly baffled as to how it could have happened. Last week a contact of mine gave me the name of a soldier who took part in the battle but has now returned to England. I

went to meet this man at a secret location and spent some hours piecing together his version of events. (He has decided to remain anonymous for reasons that will become obvious.) This is a transcript of the strange and fascinating story he told me.

Yes, mate! It really did look like we were done for. The Germans were coming at us in their thousands and there seemed to be no end to them. I don't know why it was but, as I shouldered my rifle and took aim at the advancing enemy, I suddenly remembered a little restaurant that I'd once eaten at in London. It was a vegetarian place and I'd had these cutlets made from lentils and nuts. They were supposed to taste like steak ... but they didn't! When I'd finished them

and was wiping my plate with a chunk of bread I noticed that there was a picture of Saint George killing the dragon in the middle of it. It was blue and round the edge of the plate were these words in Latin: Adsit Anglis Sanctus Georgius.

Now, I happened to have done a bit of Latin at school, so I knew that they meant: May Saint George Be Present To Help The English. For some strange reason, just as I let fire at the German soldiers, I spoke those very words. Yes, just like that! "May

Saint George Be Present To Help The English!"

Next thing I knew I felt something just like a big electric shock go right through my body and a second later the terrible roar of the battle sort of died right down to just a distant murmur. And straight after that I heard a huge voice, or rather, thousands of voices, all shouting the words: "Saint George! Saint George!" and "Ha! Messire; ha! sweet Saint, grant us good deliverance!"

The shouting was louder than thunder and I can tell you it made my insides go all wobbly and the hairs on the back of my neck stand on end! And then the strangest thing of all happened. A few yards in front of our trench a long line of misty shapes suddenly appeared as if from nowhere. There were hundreds of them and they were all shimmering and silvery and holding enormous bows of the kind that I have only ever seen before in history books and museums. They had their arrows in place and their bow strings were drawn back at the ready.

All of a sudden they all gave a great shout of "St George! Heaven's Knight, aid us!" and let their arrows go. There was a huge WHOOOOSH sound and the air was suddenly filled with a huge cloud of arrows zinging their way towards the German lines.

Strange thing is, my mates in the trench didn't seem to have noticed any of this at all and were just carrying on firing, doing their best to down the enemy, even though it seemed pointless. Then all at once a chap just down the trench from me shouts, "By jingo, look at that! We must be better shots than we thought. The enemy are going down like flies. Look! Look! More than two hundred must have fallen just while I've been speaking!" And his mate next to him, who was still firing, yelled, "Whatever are you going on about, Bert? Just shut up and shoot!" But even as that man spoke his eyes went wide with amazement because at this point the German troops were going down in their

thousands and now even he could see them!

Even so those Germans kept on coming. We could see their officers urging them on and heard the crack of pistol fire as they shot any who tried to turn back. And still they continued to fall. I've never seen anything like it in my life. And all the time this was going on I could hear that spine-tingling, ghostly yell of "Harow! Harow! Monseigneur St George, succour us!" By now the air was so thick with flying arrows that they almost blotted out the light. And then suddenly the enemy stopped coming. The ones that weren't dead or fatally wounded all turned in one great grey mass and started running back towards their lines, leaving the battlefield littered with their fallen mates. And we all let out a huge cheer. I cannot describe to you the relief we felt. There were tears in my eyes and those of my pals. I swear that all I have told you is the truth.

That is what the soldier told me. And reader, I believed him. Of course, you must make up your own mind. But don't forget! Truth is often ... stranger than fiction!

Footnote: Arthur Machen wrote this story after hearing a radio report about the awful Battle of Mons, where the British took such a terrible pounding from the Germans. Mons was quite near Agincourt, the place where King Henry V's bowmen had scored an amazing victory over the French, 500 years earlier. This connection no doubt gave Arthur the idea for his brilliant story which he had published in the *London Evening News* in September 1914.

At that time everyone at home was feeling down in the dumps about their prospects in the war so the tale's suggestion that the ghosts of the bowmen had returned to save the doomed Tommies really caught many people's imaginations. So much so that some of them actually began to believe Arthur's story was true! Then even more people began to believe the story, especially when soldiers who'd been at the battle began claiming *they'd* actually seen the ghostly bowmen! Some even said they'd examined the Germans' bodies and found arrow wounds in them! The ghostly rescuers soon became known as the Angels of Mons and all sorts of stories began to go around about them. As a result, Arthur suddenly found himself being accused of taking a *true* story and turning it into *fiction* for his own profit. Crazy or what! Even though he denied the accusations over and over again the poor chap was eventually given the sack from the *Evening News*!

The final twist in this strange tale of fiction being turned into truth came 12 years after the end of World War One. In 1930, the chief of the German wartime espionage (that's spying and whatnot) claimed that everybody had got the wrong end of the stick and that the Angels of Mons were really the creation of his "dirty tricks" department. He helpfully explained that aeroplanes carrying movie cameras had projected images of the "angels" on to clouds above the battlefields to prove to everyone that God was on the side of the Germans. Pull the other one, Fritz, it's got little wings on!

MOVIE CAMERAS INDEED !! ...ER ... WHAT ARE *THEY* ?!!

My Night of Terror by Terry Fide

It's not too hard to plant the idea of a ghost in people's minds. Once that's done their imagination does the rest! Sometimes you don't even have to sow the seeds of fear. Circumstances will do it for you! People who think they've seen a ghost often interpret quite ordinary events as being deeply sinister and supernatural! Perhaps the real art of ghostbusting is to be able to identify commonplace occurrences so that you can eliminate them, then concentrate on tackling the *truly* spooky stuff!

Here's a Mr Terry Fide's account of his "night of terror" at a holiday cottage. Read his acccount of his "ordeal" and see how many innocent explanations you can come up with for what *he* took to be truly scary events. Then check the list at the end, for a more likely story!

It was the first (and last, as it turned out) night of my winter holiday, and I wasn't feeling too happy. I'd spent a pleasant enough evening chatting to the locals in the Fib and Ferret but unfortunately, just five minutes after I'd left, my car had broken down and I'd had to abandon it. I was now walking the last three lonely miles along the unlit by-way that led to my isolated holiday cottage. Not really the sort of thing you want to be doing on a dark and stormy, freezing January night!

I'd just reached the road junction known as Dead Man's Cross when I got the strange feeling I wasn't alone. And then I saw it! Floating across the road, not four metres in front of me, was a *head*! No body, *just* a head, pale and spectral in the moonlight. And then my blood turned to ice as I remembered how they'd told me in the pub that a murderer had once been beheaded at this spot. A *murderer* who was said to have used a length of rope to throttle to death the lonely occupant of a nearby cottage one freezing January night in the seventeenth century. And *yes*, you've guessed it! It was the cottage now known as Miller's Corpse Cottage. The isolated holiday home that I was now hurrying back to!

As a gasp of terror escaped my lips, the head disappeared. Moments later I heard a muffled thump, like an axe hitting bone, then a low distant roar, like that of a cheering mob at an execution ... after which the whole night sky was suddenly lit by an eerie glow!

I turned up my collar against the biting wind and quickened my pace in a desperate attempt to get to the cottage before I should meet any more horrors. I'd almost reached my destination and was just passing the small wood which stands next to the cottage when I heard a series of blood-chilling screams come from deep within the trees. They were followed by a sound that

I can only describe as a "death rattle". The hairs on the back of my neck all rose as one as I recalled being told that the horrible murder had actually taken place in *this* wood.

It had now begun to snow heavily and was colder than ever so it was with relief that I opened the cottage door and felt the warm air rush out to greet me. As quickly as I could, I bolted the door, raced upstairs, threw off my clothes and dived into the bed. However, although I was exhausted, the horrid memory of that severed head continued to plague me and kept me awake for some time. Especially as I had just remembered the locals' comments about the cottage being "haunted by the spirits of both the strangler *and* his victim"! Nevertheless, I did eventually fall into a shallow and uneasy sleep.

I could have only been asleep for twenty minutes or so when I was woken by the most unearthly moaning and wailing I have *ever* heard in my whole life. There was no doubt about it! Some demented soul was outside the cottage screaming and howling for all they were worth. Terror stricken, I pulled the bed covers up to my chin and stared into the impenetrable blackness of the bedroom. All of a sudden those unearthly howls were joined by a desperate scraping sound from somewhere down below, like someone, or some "thing", scrabbling or scratching at a window or door in an attempt to prise it open. It was soon followed by a series of rattles and squeaks, then a long drawn out creak just like an old door makes when it swings on its rusty hinges. Surely it couldn't be someone coming into the cottage? Could it?

Beginning to feel like I would die from fear I pulled the bed covers completely over my own head! It was at this point that I heard foosteps on the stairs and knew for certain that I was in terrible danger! As I lay trembling from head to toe I heard three distinct knocks on the bedroom wall just next to me. They were shortly followed by three more. Then three more! Almost mad with fear, I sprang from the bed and instantly became aware that the room was now in the icy grip of the sinister chill or "cold spot" that is said to accompany many phantoms!

I quickly grabbed my torch from the bedside table and switched it on in readiness to make my escape. As its pale beam wavered and danced in my trembling fist something caught my eye. Slumped on the floor in the far corner of the bedroom ... lay a body! A body so horrendously twisted and mutilated that I knew it must have died in utmost agony. And at that moment I caught a whiff of the most disgusting stench I had ever smelled in my life and knew that the terrible odour that was now making my stomach heave was that of ... rotting human flesh! I had no doubt of it! The mangled heap I was looking at was ... *Miller's corpse!*

Almost fainting with fear, I burst from the room, took the stairs two at a time, and ran out of the back door into the cold night air. Free at last. But I was mistaken! He, or *it*, must have been waiting for me. As I raced across the small backyard I was suddenly stopped dead in my tracks. At first I was confused as to what could have done this, then I felt searing pain on my throat and realized that unseen hands were holding a rope across my windpipe preventing me from moving forwards. It was him, the phantom strangler!

In blind panic I thrashed and struggled but the more I fought the more the rough cord bit into my neck! I was *completely* at his mercy. It was only when I sank to the ground sobbing to be spared that I felt him release his terrible grip. I took my chance, jumped to my feet and raced off into the night, screaming until I thought my lungs would burst!

My last memory of that hellish place is seeing those spectral footprints all about me in the fresh snow and hearing that mocking laughter echoing round the woods. I knew then, that I'd only just escaped *with my life*!

Dear Mr Fide,

Perhaps when you have read the following you may want to title your account: "My Night Of ... Error!" But don't feel too bad, we all mistakes, don't we? It's just that some people make *a lot* more than others!

• You'd just spent an evening at the Fib and Ferret. A pub where the regulars' favourite pastime is questioning strangers, then telling them porkies. How do you think it got its name? Their speciality is ghost stories. It's quite obvious to us that they succesfully got *you* all of a jitter before you even left the pub!

• The so-called bodyless head you witnessed at the crossroads was actually a Mr Ernest Weedle, a nightclub bouncer from a nearby town. He'd stopped there to, er ... relieve himself. You only saw his head because he was wearing black evening dress.

• The dull thump like the sound of an axe on bone was the sound of Mr Weedle shutting his car door. The low roar was his car engine starting and the eerie light was the reflected glow of his car headlights on the clouds.

• The screams you heard were those of a little owl (or screech owl), a bird that is quite common in this area. The death rattle was the call of a night jar – a nocturnal bird that is now very rare apart from certain areas, including the one you chose for your holiday.

• You were woken by the sound of the wind blowing through the drainpipes of the cottage. Do you remember what a terrible gale was blowing that night?

• The scraping and scrabbling sounds were made by the mice that inhabit the cottage. They're a constant nuisance in many country dwellings.

• The footsteps you heard were actually the wood of the stairs contracting as the temperature dropped – remember the heating had been on most of the day!

• And those knocks on the wall were just rattles from the pipes of the central-heating system itself. The local plumber is bit of a bodger!

• The so-called "cold spot" that you were so concerned about was nothing more than the air cooling down after the central heating had gone off. Rooms do have a tendency to do this on freezing winter nights!

• Now to that body in the corner. That was your clothes which you'd so hurriedly thrown off before you jumped into bed. You certainly gave Miss Timmins, our district nurse, a surprise when she found you running along the lane absolutely starkers!

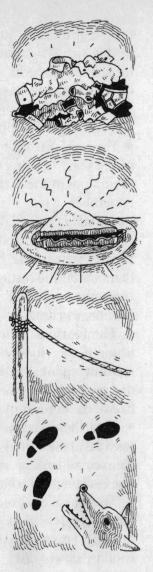

• Oh yes ... that smell of rotting human flesh that you caught a whiff of. Well yes, it *was* flesh, but it wasn't human! It came from an old corn-beef sandwich that a previous occupant of the cottage had left under the bed!

• The strangler in the dark. Well, when you arrived you may have noticed that a washing line had been left strung across the backyard. But you obviously forgot all about it in your panic!

• The footprints were the ones that you'd made earlier in the evening and the "mad laughter" was the eerie sound of a vixen barking in the little wood (or copse) next to the cottage. The one it gets its name from ... Miller's Copse!

How Fear Departed from the Long Gallery

Next up is this terrific haunted-house tale: "How Fear Departed from the Long Gallery" (1912) by E F Benson (1867-1940). It's a haunted house with a difference, though, because the Peverils, the family who live in it, aren't in the slightest bit bothered about their resident spooks, most of whom are their ancestors anyway. However, there are a couple of ghosts who do cause them and their various guests to shiver and shudder. And with good reason, as you'll soon find out! Just like many families who've lived in the same big posh country house for generations, the Peverils are the proud owners of an enormous collection of paintings. These show off past and present members of the family *and* the family pile itself (which is what mega-posh folk like to call their house). The best way to enjoy this spooky story would probably be to take a wander around the Long Gallery itself, have a squiz at the pics, and find out…

How the other half haunt

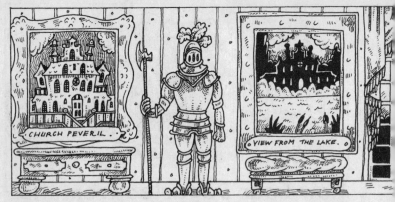

CHURCH PEVERIL .

. VIEW FROM THE LAKE .

Church Peveril, Yorkshire Church Peveril has been the home of the Yorkshire Peverils for so long that it seems as if they've lived there *for ever*! It's an enormous old country house, so vast that its green, copper-covered roofs actually cover *one and a half acres*! There are so *many* rooms that they're almost impossible to count. They include lots of draughty, candle-lit chambers with beds the size of life-rafts and ancient tapestry wall-hangings that mysteriously flap and billow at the most unexpected moments! Outside there's a tree-lined drive, gigantic gardens *and* a whopping great lake.

The Long Gallery This is where the action of our story (some of it quite *horrible*, some not *quite* so horrible) takes place. It's 80-feet long and is lit by six tall windows which overlook the gardens. Its main feature is an enormous open fireplace above which hangs a portrait of handsome Dick Peveril. (More on him later!) Its other walls are hung with dozens more portraits of Peverils past and present. There is a door at one end which leads to the landing at the top of the main staircase. Halfway along is

another door which leads to the back stairs and the servants' quarters. The long gallery has always been a popular sitting room for the Peverils and their guests (well, during the *daytime* anyway!), and its many window seats give great views of the grounds and gardens.

Mrs Peveril Mrs Peveril isn't the slightest bit bothered by ghosts. She says that at Church Peveril they get them like other people get postmen. They turn up almost every day and announce their arrival with knocks, rattles and all sorts of other commotions. So, *generally* speaking, she's never given two hoots about spooks, apart from ... er... (Well, more of them later!)

Aunt Barbara Peveril (The Blue Lady) As more perceptive readers will have noticed, Aunt Barbara is a *ghost*. She's always dressed in blue but no one's sure why. People who've see her say she's forever looking as if she wants to say something but whenever anyone asks her what it is she's after she just points ... "somewhere towards the house"!

Blanche Peveril (Mrs P's daughter)   Like her mum, Blanche has never been the slightest bit afraid of spooks apart from ... *you* don't yet know who. (But you will!) In fact she finds Aunt Barbara "a bit of a bore". She reckons that Aunt Barbara actually wants to confess some awful thing she did 200 years ago but for the life of her the dotty old thing can't remember what it was! She also thinks Aunt Barbara's dress sense is terrible and wonders what on earth made her choose such a silly shade of blue!

The Peveril's pack of pet daschunds   Not at all frightened of ghosts (or postmen!). Flo, the friskiest one, enjoys chasing Aunt Barbara around the shrubbery.

Great-great-grandmamma Bridget   Bridget appears by the fireplace in various bedrooms every now and again in a ... "vague" sort of way. Apparently she led rather a "wild" life crammed with "amazing" incidents. In the end she lost her cool with some distant relation and cut their throat after which she felt so terrible that she

disembowelled herself with one of the axes that had actually been used at the Battle of Agincourt! She's harmless, but it's best not to speak to her if you see her.

Master Anthony Peveril Master Anthony was a right ruffian *and* extremely "vulgar". Like all the Peverils he was barmy about the outdoor life and loved hunting and shooting and golf and skating and whatnot! One day when he was feeling particularly adventurous he tried to ride his horse up the main staircase at Church Peveril. The horse didn't like this and threw a wobbly. The other thing it threw was Master Anthony who landed on his bonce, broke his neck and died! At night you can still hear him having yet another go at clip-clopping his way up the staircase.

Master Joseph Peveril Master Joseph lived at around the same time as Queen Elizabeth I. He was the owner of Church Peveril and all the family lands. In 1600 he became a father to twin boys, aged 74! (Him, not the twins!)

DICK PEVERIL.

THE Peveril Twins

Dick Peveril Dick was the much younger brother of Joseph. He was wickedly handsome and handsomely wicked (but in a very *ugly* way, of course). One day Queen Elizabeth I said to him, "What a pity you are not master of Church Peveril." This put an idea into his head and led to some very nasty goings on indeed!

The Peveril twins These were the lovely children of Joseph. When they were aged just two years old and hardly able to talk or walk, their dad *also* began to find these two activities a bit difficult, and soon afterwards he died from drinking too much sweet sherry. Along with lots of other far-flung Peverils, wicked Uncle Dick came to Church Peveril to pay his last respects to Joseph. Then, a few nights after his brother's funeral, Dick snuck into the twins' bedroom just next door to the Long Gallery where they lay sleeping peacefully alongside their nurse. As quickly and quietly as he could, Dick strangled the nurse. Now for the *really* horrible bit! Ready? Are you sure you can take this? Oh, all right then, suit yourself, here goes! Wicked Dick

UNLUCKY SERVANT

lifted the twins out of their cot and carried them into the Long Gallery. He scooped out a space in the middle of the huge log fire that was blazing furiously in the meganormous fireplace then, without any hesitation, he threw the twins into it. After giving them a good stamping down with his size 12 riding boots, he added more logs to the fire just to make sure they were well and truly cooked. It is said that he laughed as he did all this! No one ever suspected that it was Dick who'd done this dastardly deed and he soon became master of Church Peveril just like he wanted! However, after ruling the place for just one year, he fell fatally ill. (Nowhere near soon enough!) As he lay on his death bed he confessed his crime but died before the priest had time to grant him forgiveness (or give him a well-deserved smack in the mouth!).

The unlucky servant Two hours after Dick's death this poor chap was passing the Long Gallery when he heard peals of loud laughter coming from it. It was joyful yet sinister and he recognized it immediately as that of

wicked Dick! With a mixture of terror, courage, curiosity and whatever else he happened to be feeling at that moment he opened the door and entered, expecting to come face to face with the ghost of devilish Dick! But he didn't! Toddling towards him, glowing eerily in the pale moonlight that was flooding in through the six big windows, were the *twins*! They were dressed in their nightshirts and holding hands. So great was his shock that he slumped to the floor.

Startled by the crash, the Peverils, who'd been sitting in the room below, raced upstairs to find him writhing around having some sort of convulsion! He survived the night and just before dawn he regained consciousness and told his awful tale! Then, raising a trembling finger that had turned to the colour of ash, he pointed to the dreaded door of the Long Gallery, gave an almighty scream and fell back ... dead as a recently deceased domestic!

During the next 50 years or so the twins appeared to people another four or five times. *Always* at night and *always* as toddlers who could hardly walk! Whoever saw them *always* died quickly ... or awfully ... or *both*!

Mrs Canning Mrs Canning was glamorous and famous and clever(ish). If she'd lived nowadays she'd be forever appearing on TV chat shows, flashing her "day-glo" teeth and being "cute". She was also what is known as a sceptic, which means she didn't believe in ghosts or the supernatural or any other such codswallop, as she would have described it. In 1760 she visited Church Peveril as a house guest and, despite all warnings, she deliberately went and sat in the Long Gallery during the hours of darkness.

For four nights she saw nothing, then on the fifth night the door in the middle of the gallery opened and, looking as innocent as the day they were born and holding each other's little hands, in toddled those lovely twins. Being the sort of woman she was, Mrs Canning wasn't in the slightest bit frightened. She even went as far as to tease the twins and to tell them that it was about time they were *getting back in the fire*! (Can you believe the *nerve* of the hard-hearted thing, not to mention her bad taste!) This upset the poor little things so much that they began to sob their socks off and a few moments later they disappeared. Mrs Canning rushed

downstairs all excited and full of herself to tell the family of her "triumph", as she called it!

Up until this point, 1760 had been a great year for Mrs Canning. She was mind-bogglingly beautiful and was definitely looking her most stunningest ever! One of her best features was her complexion. She had skin like "peaches and cream" which glowed with health and beauty and made all other women jealous as anything. But about two weeks after meeting the twins Mrs Canning noticed a small greyish-green patch of skin about the size of a bottle top on her previously flawless fizzog.

A week later it had doubled in size, despite all her efforts to get rid of it! Not long after this, small greenish-grey tendrils sprouted from the middle of it (a bit like you get on the lichen which you find on country walls). Then another similar patch appeared on her lower lip. One morning she woke to find she couldn't see very well out of one eye and when she looked in the mirror she saw that another grey spot had sprung up on her eye just under the lid and the tendril thingies were

hanging down over her eyeball. Next her tongue and throat were attacked by the fungus.

Two weeks later she was as dead as a dish of dessicated dinosaur, having suffocated when her windpipe became completely blocked with the horrible green "licheny" stuff. (Reader, do please *stop* feeling your cheek and fiddling with your flipping tongue!)

Colonel Blantyre When crusty Colonel Blantyre met the twins he was daft enough to fire his revolver at them. As a result he suffered a death which was *far* worse than that of Mrs Canning ... so horrible that it cannot be written down here! But no doubt *you* will use your *own* disgustingly warped and twisted imagination to conjure up a suitably horrendous scenario, you little ghoul, you! After the terrible end of the dippy colonel and all the other unfortunate souls who'd bumped into the twins it became normal for the Peveril family and their house guests to avoid the Long Gallery after sunset. The daylight hours were fine but woe betide any dimwit who lingered there during the hours of darkness!

Madge Dalrymple Madge Dalrymple, who was Blanche Peveril's first cousin, was a guest at one of the Peverils' famous house parties. It was Christmas and the big lake was frozen solid. Everyone was having lots of fun skating but poor Madge had fallen and injured her knee. As she didn't want to be out of action for the dance that evening she decided to spend the rest of the day reading her book in the Long Gallery. The sofa she was sitting on was covered in greyish-green velvety material which reminded her no end of the licheny growth stuff which had done for Mrs Canning. Well, what with the cheery fire and being plumb tuckered out with the skating, in no time at all Madge nodded off. And the last thought she'd had in her head was of that horrible stuff that had covered Mrs Canning.

She soon began to dream and in her dream she was still on the sofa and the fire was blazing merrily, lighting up the handsome (but dastardly) Dick's eyes in his portrait, and Madge was thinking she must go and write a couple of letters, but when she tried to stand up she couldn't. She looked down at her arms which were lying out at either side of her on the greenish-grey sofa and she saw that the ends

of them (or "hands" as they're usually called) had sort
of "melted" into the sofa material and become part of it!
With horror, she realized that she was being taken over
by the stuff and if she didn't do something soon she'd
just be a big lump of greenish-grey sofa material! So she
did ... she woke up!

She felt quite relieved at first but this didn't last long
because when she looked down at her hands she
couldn't see them! That's when she realized it was
almost dark! With a terrible, terrible panic that was even
worse than the one she'd had in her dream she suddenly
knew that she was about to see ... *the twins*! Her mouth
went dry and her tongue suddenly felt as if it was *glued*
to the roof of her mouth! She felt frozen by fear but she
forced herself to stand up and walk towards the door.
However, no matter which way she turned, she seemed
to be blocked by different pieces of furniture which
appeared to have rearranged themselves in the darkness,
blocking her escape entirely!

Suddenly the dying embers of the fire flared up and
she saw that she was facing the door through which the

twins usually made their entrance. Then she heard a whisper and saw the handle of the door begin to turn. The door opened and in the opening there appeared two little figures dressed in white! They came towards her, shuffling the way that toddlers do, and when they were just inches away from her Madge sank to her knees in front of them. She thought of their innnocent little spirits and the terrible thing that had happened to them and how they brought death and terror to people even though they probably didn't want to and how it was all *such* a pity because little children are supposed to bring happiness to people, not terror and fungus, so she said, "Oh, my dears, forgive me. I didn't mean to be here after dark but I fell asleep. And I am so so sorry for you both, my dears. Bless you, my little darlings."

And then she saw that they were smiling their shy baby smiles at her and as they did they began fading like the mist does when the sun comes out on crisp autumn mornings and soon they were gone! And after that Madge felt surrounded by a feeling of complete happiness and all the pain suddenly went from her crook leg.

She left the Long Gallery and a moment later she bumped into Blanche who'd just come in from skating. "How's the jolly old leg, old thing, what?" asked Blanche. Madge told her it was completely better and that she'd just seen the twins. When she said this Blanche blanched as white as a snowflake and said, "Jolly cripes, old thing! *What!*" and good, sensitive Madge said, "Yes, I saw them a moment ago and they were kind and smiling and I felt sorry for them. And now I just *know* that I've got *nothing* to fear." And she was right because after that the curse of the twins just melted away.

Nowadays Blanche says to people, "Oh by the way, I saw the twins the other day. They looked ever so sweet and they stayed a whole quarter of an hour. Do you fancy a game of golf?"

A trio of "real" haunted houses

One: Glamis Castle

Glamis Castle was built in the fourteenth century and is the oldest inhabited castle in Scotland (in fact, the Queen's sister, Princess Margaret, was born there). In addition to having so many spooks that they're falling over each other it's also said to have had its own monster *and* its own vampire!

The ghost of Lord "Beardie" Crawford

Beardie was fond of a gamble but one day he couldn't get anyone to play with him. As luck would have it the Devil happened to turn up and say, "'Ere, fungus face! I'll give you a game of dice!" or words to that effect. Beardie didn't give two hoots who he played dice with, so he said, "All right, spikey bonce!" or something of that sort.

Later on, him and the Devil got to arguing and the Devil cursed him, which caused him to die five years later and become a big hairy ghost who still stamps around and rattles his dice.

The unlucky Ogilvys

The Ogilvy family came to Glamis to ask for protection against the Lindsays who'd just whupped them in a clan feud. "Of course! Be our guest!" said the then Earl of Glamis. "You can hide in one of our rooms. We've got *hundreds*! But I'll lock you in just to be on the safe side." Then he promptly forgot all about them! As a result of the Earl of MacDimwit's mistake the poor Ogilvys starved to death and it's said that their ghosts can still be heard hammering and banging to be let out.

The tongueless woman

This ghost runs around tearing at her mouth. Apparently she's got far less to say for herself than the Ogilvys.

Jack the runner

Jack's a very thin ghost who races up and down the drive a lot (which is probably why he's so thin).

The ghost of Janet Douglas

When her hubby, the 6th Earl of Glamis, died an "early" death just after eating his breakfast, Janet was suspected of poisoning him. And six years after that, her reputation as a cereal killer was confirmed when she was accused of murdering King James V. As a result she became the toast of the nation, or to put it another way, she was burned at the stake. Her ghost now appears in flames or wrapped in a reddish glow.

The self-opening door
Nailing it, locking it, jamming snake-shaped draught-excluders under it ... *nothing* will stop this door from opening on its own.

The hairy heir
According to legend, the first son of the 11th Earl was completely egg-shaped and covered all over with hair so he was kept in a secret chamber. In 1865 a workman accidentally knocked through a wall, found the secret passage that led to the chamber and got a shock! Not long after this the workman mysteriously disappeared! It was said that he'd been given some money and sent to Australia so that he wouldn't spill the beans about the "monster"... as Eggbert was so *unkindly* called. The bit of the castle where the hairy heir was "eggsercised" is known as "The Mad Earl's Walk"! (Probably because he was slightly cracked.)

The ghost of the black boy
This boy is said to sit by the door to the Queen Mother's sitting room. It's thought that he was a page who may have been badly treated (or just torn off a strip or two).

The vampire maid

A servant at the castle was once caught sucking the blood of a guest so as a punishment she was walled up alive (and fined three weeks' wages).

The phantom bloodstain

This bloodstain was amazing and spooky and weird because no matter how hard it was scrubbed at it just wouldn't go away. In the end the floor had to be boarded over to hide it. But what is even more amazing is that the blood is said to be that of King Duncan of Scotland who was murdered by Macbeth in the eleventh century – which was about 300 years before Glamis Castle was actually built!

Two: Ballechin House

Major Stuart had lived in India for a long time but he didn't fancy spending his retirement there, so in 1850 he returned home to Ballechin House in Scotland where he could live out his twilight years with his beloved dogs, of which he'd got loads!

The major believed in something called the transmigration of the soul. (Quite simply this means that when you die your soul flits out of your own body and into someone else's body or something else that is already around. Could be a pop star, cuddly toy, paper clip, banana ... whatever you fancy really!) As the major was absolutely crazy about dogs it occured to him that it would be rather nice to come back dog-shaped. He didn't have any children of his own so he decided he'd have to tell John, his grown-up nephew, and his family of his brilliant plan because it was them who would be inheriting his fab house and groovy dogs.

So he got them all together and said, "Now listen here, everyone. ATTENSHUN! I've decided that when I turn up my toes I'm going to come back and live in the body of my favourite cocker-spaniel. OK! You're all ... DISMISSED!" or something like that. The family were appalled – the last thing they wanted was to have Uncle Loony ... sorry, Major Stuart ... bouncing around inside a spaniel and sticking his nose into everyone else's business (so to speak). So, when he did finally die in 1876 they stood all of his lovely dogs in front of a firing squad and had the paw things shot!

Of course, this was *asking* for trouble! Well, where would the major's soul go if it didn't have a nice warm live dog to snuggle up inside of? Pet Rescue? Battersea Dogs' Home? Rolf Harris's cardigan? No way, Fido! So, of course, the major's soul was back like a shot. And it was barking mad! (Well, it would be, wouldn't it.) For the next 20 years the family were dogged by all sorts of weird and scary goings on.

John's wife was forever smelling dogs in his study. She sometimes felt an invisible dog pushing against her legs. Servants left because of all the rappings, groans and ghostly cold patches in the house. The family were hounded by a phantom black spaniel. Whimpering sounds and the noise of a dog's tail bashing against doors could be heard at all hours of the day and night. (Don't you just *hate it* when they do that?)

One night John's wife was woken by the sound of her own dog whimpering. She looked on the bedside table and saw a pair of disembodied dog paws (or "woolly mittens" as normal people call them).

Then the final terrible blow came! Just before he was due to go to London one day John was on the phone when he heard three loud knocks. In the world of ghosts this is a sign that something bad is about to happen. When John arrived in the city a few hours later he was run over and killed by a taxi-cab. Perhaps the dog ghosts and the major's ghost had teamed up to get their revenge on the horrible family? Or maybe it was just the family's collective guilty conscience playing tricks on them. Anyway, whatever it was, it jolly well served them right!

I'LL SECOND THAT!

Three: Amityville, Long Island, America

It was a dream house – three storeys, a swimming pool, a beautiful lawn sloping down to the sea, and a boat house. There was only one problem. It was also a nightmare house. A young man flipped his lid and murdered his family there. So at least the Lutzes were able to buy it quite cheaply. They did! And that's when their problems began...

When they moved in the Lutzes asked a priest to "bless" the house. As he did a deep voice came from nowhere and said, "Get out!" (Maybe he'd gone next door by mistake?)

On their first and second nights in the house the Lutzes were woken by strange noises. They heard them at 3.15 a.m., the exact time that the horrible murders had taken place ... oooer!

On their third night the noises came again, so Mr Lutz went downstairs for a look round. He found the big solid front door hanging from one hinge with its lock broken.

(Had no one warned them about the giant mice?)

After that the house got *really* silly. Windows began to open and close on their own, window panes shattered, a piece of bannister leapt into the air. (It was probably tired of being staired at.)

Mr Lutz got a bit of a surprise one night when he awoke to find Mrs Lutz floating above their bed. (She was normally such a down-to-earth type.) He finally got her to land by pulling her hair.

He then noticed that her face had become utterly hideous. When she looked in the mirror she didn't recognize herself. It took her six hours to regain her normal appearance. (And six more to get Mr Lutz to come out of the cupboard!)

The Lutzes were in their sitting room having a sit when Mrs Lutz looked at the darkened window and saw two red glowing eyes staring in at her.

When they rushed outside and investigated they found tracks in the snow. They'd been made by something with cloven hooves.

Not long after this, black gunge began dribbling out of keyholes and green slime started to ooze from the walls and ceilings. (Mr Lutz was renowned for his creative bogey-flicking sessions.)

Twenty-eight days after they'd moved in the Lutzes moved out. As they left, the house was making a terrible racket. (It was obviously pleased to see them go.)

The Lutzes' experiences were so *unbelievably* terrifying that a book was written about the house and a film, *The Amityville Horror*, was made of their story. After the Lutzes had left the house of horrors another couple bought it and moved in. And *they* didn't hear a peep out of the place ... not so much as an eerie echo or a ghostly burp! Why? Because, as everyone discovered sometime later, the Lutzes had invented the whole story of the hauntings when they found they couldn't afford the upkeep of their new home. Some people!

The Night Mail

Have you ever caught a bus or a train, then realized that everyone else on it is very weird or odd in some way and that you are the only normal person on board? And then have you realized that you are actually going to be trapped inside this vehicle with all these scary characters for quite some time? That's more or less what happens to the person in the story "The Night Mail" (also known as "The Phantom Coach") by Amelia B A Edwards (1831–92). Except in this case the vehicle is a stagecoach that turns up one dark, cold night at the exact spot where years before a very "similar" stagecoach was involved in a terrible accident in which the horses, drivers and passengers were all killed.

Let's imagine that the person who's caught the coach doesn't realize he's on board a coach full of spooks and just thinks the coach company are a bit of a shambles. So what does he do after his nightmare ride? He writes to the coach company to complain, of course! By the way, don't forget to keep a body count!

A wheelly spokey story

Clueless Cottage,
Old North Road,
Fools Moor

15th March 1858

Spectral Stagecoaches Inc,
Grisly Hall,
Goole.

Dear Sir,

I am writing to complain about the despicably low standard of service I recently had to put up with whilst travelling on one of your stagecoaches. I have never had a more disagreeable, uncomfortable or "disturbing" journey in many years of travelling the highways and byways of old England. I think the memory of it will haunt me for the rest of my life! If this is the level of service you always provide for your passengers it is a wonder that you are still in business! In addition, I would also like to complain about your rude staff and about the sort of passenger you allow to use your service. Never have I come across a more horrible, disagreeable and ghastly set of human beings! But more of them later...

For you fully to understand the distress I suffered during my journey I must explain how I came to take your coach in the first place. I hope that when you have read my letter you will see fit to offer me some sort of compensation and immediately set about improving your absolutely horrendous services!

My story is as follows:

I was enjoying a short winter break with my lovely young wife in the north of England. On the second day of our holiday I decided to go for a brisk hike across the moors but she said she'd prefer to spend the day reading so I left her at the cosy inn where we were staying. I had been walking for about five hours when a blizzard unexpectedly blew up and I soon became lost. After staggering through the snowstorm for what seemed like ages I came across an old man whom I later discovered was called Jacob. When I told him of my predicament he led me to a rather large and mysterious-looking house where I met his master. He was an odd but rather interesting gentleman who kindly gave me a most welcome meal of ham and eggs and good brown bread. He was very glad of my company as he'd lived on his own for nearly thirty years and I was the first visitor he'd had in ages. After an hour or two of pleasant conversation he pulled aside the parlour curtain and said, "Ah, my friend, the snow has stopped at last!"

"In that case I must leave," I said. "I am newly married and my wife will be worried to death about me. She is 20 miles away at the inn at Dwolding and I must reach her this evening. I would pay 50 pounds for a guide and a good horse to get me there!"

"You can get there much more cheaply than that!" said the man. "The night mail from the north which passes through Dwolding is due at the crossroads on the moor in just one hour. Jacob will show you the way up to the old coach road."

I thanked the man for his kindness, then Jacob and I stepped out into the night. The wind had dropped but it was still bitterly cold. There was not a star in the black night sky and all was silent apart from the sound of the frozen snow crunching beneath our feet. After a while Jacob stopped and pointed, saying, "That there's the road you must take. Keep on for a quarter of a mile until you reach the crossroads. But mind how you go! There is a steep drop right next to the track! You'll know when you've reached the cossroads because the wall is broken away next to the signpost. It's never been mended since the accident."

"What accident?" I asked.

"It were the night mail," he replied. "Nine years ago it were taking the bend when it toppled right into the valley below!"

(So, Spectral Stagecoaches Inc, I hadn't even begun my journey and I was learning of your dreadful reputation! As well as substandard services, you have careless drivers too!)

"How awful!" I said. "Was anyone hurt?"

"Four died straightaway and two more next day!" he said. "There were no survivors. Not even the horses. But now I must take my leave of you." And with that he walked off into the night and was soon gone from my sight.

After a difficult walk I reached the spot where the wall was broken and, as I looked down into the frozen valley where those poor souls had met their deaths, I shuddered.

(But more to the point, Spectral Stagecoaches Inc, don't you think it's about time you had that dangerous broken wall mended as it was one of your coaches that caused the damage in the first place!)

I stood by the signpost for what seemed like a lifetime, anxiously checking my watch every five minutes! The old man had told me the coach was due at any time.

(Yes, that's right! Your coach was late! What pathetic excuse will you offer for that, I wonder? Broken milestone at Devil's Bridge? Horse failure on the York turnpike? The wrong sort of snow on the road over Starkbone Moor?)

As I waited, I became colder and colder. I lost all feeling in my hands. My feet were like ice. I thought I would freeze to death if I stood there much longer.

(Will you ever get around to providing shelters at your coach stops? I doubt it!)

I was just beginning to despair of ever seeing my young wife again and had almost given up the ghost when I saw a distant gleam of light. It was the coach! It was approaching the crossroads swiftly and silently. I leapt into the road and waved my hat. But as I did ... the coach sped past me!

(Spectral Stagecoaches! There is nothing more irritating than having to wait at a coach stop for absolutely ages, and then, when a coach finally does come, put out your hand for it, only to see it speed past you! Especially when it is plain to see there are seats available! I would be grateful if you would inform your drivers of this!)

Then, just as I thought I was abandoned for ever ... the coach stopped! I picked up my bag and ran to the waiting vehicle. On arriving at the door I gave a cheery greeting to the driver and his mate but was disappointed to note that both of them ignored me completely!

(Would you please explain to your employees that politeness costs nothing. All that's needed is a friendly nod or smile to the customer. You know ... just to let them know that they have been noticed ... and are valued!)

I spoke again but still they ignored me. They didn't even turn to look at me! I wondered if they had even seen me, what with them being muffled up to their eyes in blankets and scarves. And then something struck me! They both appeared to be fast asleep!

(I was appalled. I realize that driving stagecoaches over long distances is a demanding and exhausting task but there is no excuse for napping on the job. The safety of your passengers must come first! Surely your employees have seen

those roadside signs: "Tiredness can kill. Take a break!"? I really do feel it is only a matter of time before one of your vehicles is involved in another terrible disaster!)

Realizing neither of the fellows would come down to help me, I opened the door myself and entered the coach. I peered around its dark and gloomy interior and could just make out that three of the seats were already occupied so I quickly slipped into the fourth empty one. Straight away I noticed that, although it was a bitterly cold night, the air inside the coach seemed to be even colder than outside! And also quite damp and clammy! I immediately began to shiver uncontrollably.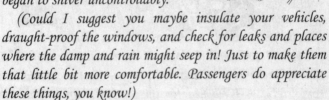

(Could I suggest you maybe insulate your vehicles, draught-proof the windows, and check for leaks and places where the damp and rain might seep in! Just to make them that little bit more comfortable. Passengers do appreciate these things, you know!)

As I settled down in my corner I became aware of a most horrible smell. I can't quite put my finger on exactly what it was, but it reminded me of a hunk of meat that's been left in a warm place for too long and has become completely foul and rotten, and most probably seething with maggots. It really was most unpleasant!

(Spectral Stagecoaches! Has it ever occurred to you to clean and air your coaches between journeys? It wouldn't go amiss, you know! Just get your cleaning staff – you do have them, don't you? – to open the windows for an hour or two, have a bit of tidy round, and remove bits of rotting, discarded food. It's not a lot to ask!)

Next I looked at my fellow passengers. They weren't asleep but they were very silent and all three of them seemed to be deep in thought. "Hmm!" I said to myself. "They're probably feeling just as miserable and upset about their choice of transport as I am!"

(And they were no doubt thinking that they too would never travel by Spectral Stagecoaches again! Not even if their very lives depended on it!)

"Cold night!" I said cheerily to the fellow opposite me. He lifted his head, but said nothing. "Winter draws on!" I quipped, hoping to bring a cheery twinkle to his eyes. But still he did not react and continued to look at me with his completely deadpan stare. At this point, that dreadful smell of rotting flesh became just too much for me to bear and I thought that I would be quite sick if I sat there much longer.

"Would you mind if I opened the window a smidge?" I said to the fellow sitting next to me. He too ignored me completely, so I reached for the leather strap to pull the window down. As I did, it broke off in my hand. It was

 completely rotted through! Then I noticed the window itself. It was covered in the most revolting green fungus, like it hadn't been cleaned for ages! Taking advantage of the faint glow that came from the outer coach lamps I began to inspect the rest of the vehicle's

interior. It was in the most terrible state of decay! The leather seats were crusted in mould! The wooden floor was so rotten that it seemed to be breaking up beneath my feet. In fact the entire vehicle looked like it had been mouldering away in some forgotten shed for years and years!

(In short, Spectral Stagecoaches, your coach wasn't fit to transport pigs in, never mind human beings! And it certainly wouldn't have passed a safety inspection. I can honestly say that it was nothing less than a death trap!)

"What a dreadful state this coach is in!" I said to the third passenger. "I suppose the regular one is in for some sort of repair and this old bone-shaker is a temporary replacement?"

As I spoke, he turned his head and looked at me. When I saw his face my heart went cold. His eyes were glowing. His skin was as pale as that of a ... of a ... corpse! And his lips were curled back so horribly that I could see all his teeth and gums. It was almost as if he were in the middle of his own agonizing death!

(Spectral stagecoaches! That poor man must have been hating every moment of his journey. And are you surprised! Do you have no regard for the well-being of your passengers? I really do feel that your neglect of passenger welfare is a most grave issue!)

I now looked at the other fellow who sat opposite me. My eyes had grown quite used to the gloom by now. What a shock I got! He had exactly the same corpse-like skin. And the same cold, glittering eyes were fixing me with the same chilling stare. I quickly turned to the passenger who was sitting next to me. And it was at that moment that I realized this was ... no living man! In fact, unlike me, none of them were living men. Their awful faces were lit by the unearthly glow that rotting flesh gives off. Their clothes were stained with mud (and things much worse) and were hanging from their bodies in tattered shreds. Their hands were the hands of corpses that have been dug from the grave. The only things about them that seemed to be properly alive were their awful eyes. The eyes that were all now staring at me!

(I am not used to travelling with this class of person. In fact I always make a point of travelling first class so that I can avoid these unpleasant types! So why do you allow them to use your service. Surely these sorts are more suited to the carrier's cart! I suggest that in future you reserve certain coaches for a better class of person, like myself!)

As those three pairs of glittering eyes continued to stare at me from those dreadful faces, I screamed in terror and hurled myself at the door of the coach, desperately pulling and tugging to get it open. At that moment the moon emerged from behind a cloud and lit the dreadful scene. I saw the sinister signpost with its beckoning finger ... the broken wall ... the horses rearing and screaming as they plunged towards the valley below ... and that great dark space opening to swallow us! The coach swung wildly; I was aware of falling into space.

Seconds later there was an almighty crash – I felt searing pain all over my body – then all went dark!

(So, Spectral Stagecoaches. I was right, wasn't I? Your drivers hadn't got their minds on the job! And look what happened. Your safety record really is appalling!)

When I eventually awoke I found myself in my own house with my wife at my bedside. As I opened my eyes she gave a sigh and squeezed my hand, telling me how relieved she was to see me regain consciousness. It felt like many years had gone by since the day of the blizzard so I asked her to tell me all that had happened. She told me how I had slipped in the snow and toppled over the valley's edge next to the signpost by the old coach road. She said I had been very lucky because a snow drift had broken my fall. Two shepherds had discovered me and called a doctor who immediately saw that I had a fractured skull and was raving deliriously. As I did not wish to worry my wife further I decided to let her believe that story and never ever to tell her of my dreadful experience (in your awful stagecoach).

After being nursed by my wife for many months I eventually recovered. As soon as I felt fit enough I went to see the doctor to discuss my compensation claim for the injuries I had suffered in the coach crash.

"What coach crash?" he replied with some astonishment. "As far as I am concerned you were walking on the valley's edge in the dark, lost your footing, then slipped and fell!"

So I told him all about your coach and your rude employees and your horrendous passengers and the crash. And he replied that I appeared to have gone completely over the top. "Yes!" I said. "I did! In that dratted coach!" And he said that was not what he meant and that I was obviously imagining all these things as a result of the brain fever I had suffered.

(But Spectral Stagecoaches Inc, we know better than that, don't we? Now that I am fully recovered I am sure that what happened to me was not just something I dreamed up! Especially as those shepherds did find me at a well-known accident blackspot where an almost identical tragedy had taken place nine years earlier. A tragedy that was also your fault! You really should be ashamed of yourselves! I will never travel in one of your coaches again. To be honest with you ... I wouldn't even be seen dead in one!)

Yours disgustedly,

A. Sixthbody

Transports of terror

Nine of these phantom transports of terror are said to have been seen by frightened folk all around the world but one of them's the subject of a story by a well-known author. Spot the odd one out!

The phantom coach of Brockley Combe
We'll start with a "real" phantom coach. This coach is said to drive up and down a lane near Brockley Combe in Somerset, pulled by four horses and driven by a headless man (how does he see where he's going?).

A man who'd heard of the ghost coach went to see it for himself. As he waited for it to appear, the scary atmosphere of the lane began to get to him, so he picked up some stones to protect himself. All of a sudden he heard the rumble of coach wheels behind him! Turning, he saw a coach coming towards him.

"Oooer ... *mother*!" he thought. "I do not like this!" (or something like that) and began bunging stones at the coach like a mad thing. Which wasn't a good idea, because it *wasn't* the phantom coach! It was a coachload of footballers who just happened to be passing along the lane on their way home from a match! The footie players were so miffed with the man that they jumped off the coach and chased him down the lane. But then just as they caught up with him ... the real phantom coach appeared and frightened the shin pads off the whole lot of them! Wow! But that's the irritating thing about "phantom" coaches isn't it – you wait for ages without any sign of one, and then they all turn up at once!

The phantom coach was also seen by a cyclist who met it head-on in the lane. He was unable to get out of its way and next moment he felt a horrible chill all over his body as it passed right through him!

The *Flying Dutchman*

There are lots of versions of this ghost-ship story so if you go looking for it you'll probably meet a whole fleet of them with their ghostly captains all knocking the ectoplasm out of each other in a scrap to prove who's in charge of the genuine article!

Basically the *Flying Dutchman* is a ship that's been condemned to sail the really stroppy bit of sea known as the Cape of Good Hope (ha ha) for ever and ever because: (Delete as applicable or just pick 'n' mix.)

a) Its *Dutch* captain, van Straaten, stubbornly said he would sail round the Cape despite waves the size of shopping malls. Not long after this the captain and crew went to bed ... the *sea*bed!

b) Its *German* captain, von Falkenberg, lost his soul to the Devil in a game of dice and was made to sail for ever as a forfeit.

c) Its *British* captain was determined to rule the waves and he shook his fist at God, challenging him to sink the ship. In response to this an apparition appeared on deck. The captain tried to shoot it but his gun exploded in his hand. Just to add insult to injury the apparition cursed him to sail for ever ... so there!

d) Its *other* Dutch captain, Van der Decken, said to the Devil, "You can have my soul if you let me round the Cape!" and the Devil pulled a fast one on him by saying, "OK!" but *not* telling him that he would be capering round the Cape for ever! Well, what else did the chump *expect* from someone as deeply dodgy as the devil!

WELL... YA GOTTA 'AVE A BIT OF FUN, 'AVEN'T YA ?!

The tale is generally known as the legend of the "Flying Dutchman" because that's what imaginative and over-excitable German composer Richard Wagner decided to call the opera he wrote after being inspired by all these tales of sails and spooks.

Warning: If you do happen to spot the *Flying Dutchman*, close your eyes immediately! Many people who are said to have seen it become cursed with bad luck.

Flight 401

In 1973, American Eastern Airlines Flight 401 was flying over swampland in Florida when the pilot, Captain Loft, noticed a problem. Captain Loft put the plane under the control of its automatic pilot so that he and Don Repo, the flight engineer, could investigate the fault. Unfortunately, while they were busy checking out the problem, Captain Loft accidentally knocked the automatic pilot switch causing it to de-activate. This meant that no one was actually flying the aeroplane! By the time Captain Loft noticed the error it was too late to do anything about it. The plane crashed into the swamp killing the crew and 100 of the passengers.

When the rescue services finally managed to pull the wreckage from the swamp they found that some of it was undamaged. "Waste not, want not!" thought the airline, and in order to save a dollar or three they returned the bits and pieces to the aeroplane manufacturers so they could be used in other aeroplanes. (Uh oh!)

Not long after this, extremely weird things began happening aboard the planes that had been fitted out with Flight 401's bits and bobs. For starters (and despite the fact that no one had actually *fitted* him at the factory) Captain Loft himself turned up on a flight and began chatting to one of the passengers!

Then a flight engineer on another flight discovered Don Repo sitting in his seat just before take off. Don's ghost said something like, "No need to check the instruments, buddy, I've already done it for you." Which *was* nice of him, wasn't it?

Captain Loft and Don started materializing all over the place and soon people generally began to get the impression that the spooks were going out of their way to be helpful, especially when Don popped up on one plane and said to the pilot, "There will never be another crash on this type of aeroplane. *We* will not let it happen."

Not all the pilots welcomed the presence of these "helpful" spooks on their planes. Which isn't surprising really, when you think back to Don and Captain Loft's little "problem" with Flight 401! One pilot was so upset by the experience that he sprinkled water (probably holy) around his aeroplane, then said a few prayers. Maybe something like, "Look chaps, we really *do* appreciate your concern for our safety but will you please ... *go away*!" Anyway, whatever he said must have really upset the supportive spooks because they were never seen again! Some people just don't appreciate a helping hand when they're offered one, do they?

The ghost train of the Tay Bridge

On a wild and stormy late December's night in 1879 (just listen to that gale ... woo woo!) the wind was so strong that it blew down the middle section of the enormous metal railway bridge that spans the river Tay in Scotland. The Edinburgh to Dundee night train was just about to cross it! (Woo woo! That's the train now, not the gale.) Unfortunately the driver had no way of knowing that the bit of bridge he was planning to whizz across in just seconds had recently been replaced by a much less reliable stretch of thin air and the train plunged straight into the river, killing the crew and all

78 of the passengers. Not long afterwards rumours began to go around that the bridge was haunted by the ghosts (woo woo!) of the people who'd been killed.

Eight years later the repaired bridge was re-opened but the rumours continued. Then, one wild and stormy *late December's night* (yes, you might have known it!) a man was gazing up at the bridge (some people do have strange hobbies, don't they?) when he saw a completely silent train rush across it and disappear at the very spot where the accident had taken place. Woo woo ... woo ... splosh!

President Lincoln's funeral train

There are lots of spooky stories associated with President Abraham Lincoln of the USA. After he was assassinated at a theatre in Washington in 1865 his body was sent on a last trip across America. Ever since then the train is said to repeat the journey at exactly the same moment each year. (So there *is* a train that runs on time.)

Whenever the ghostly black train passes through a station the clocks all stop. (And that's how they do it!) Lincoln's never been seen on the train but a band of skeleton musicians have been spotted on one of the wagons. (The bandwagon, presumably.)

The mysterious *Mary Celeste*

Unlike the *Flying Dutchman* this ghost ship could actually be seen and touched. It was found floating in the middle of the Atlantic Ocean on 14 November 1872. Everything was in perfect order. The sails were set. There was washing on the washing line. The table was laid for breakfast of boiled eggs and all the trimmings. The captain's personal boiled egg even had its top neatly sliced off, ready for him to dip his little bread soldiers into it. The only thing that

THIS IS EGGS-TREMELY SPOOKY!

was missing were people. All the passengers and crew had disappeared! There was no sign of a storm or a mutiny or any sort of kerfuffle whatsoever. So why had the nine crew and the captain's family vanished? Boiled eggs for breakfast aren't *that* bad!

The celestial omnibus of Surbiton

A boy who lived in the London suburb of Surbiton during the nineteenth century saw a signpost with the words "To heaven" painted on it. Next to it was a sign and timetable for an omnibus company. At sunset he went to the spot and just as he'd hoped there was the omnibus with two horses still steaming from their journey.

He caught the bus and travelled through the sky on it, seeing many amazing sights before returning to earth. When he got home and told everyone about his amazing experience his dad walloped him for telling lies. However, his dad's pal got all excited about the idea and secretly asked the boy to prove he was telling the truth by taking him on the coach with him next time he went for a spin. They caught the coach but halfway through the journey the man threw a wobbly and rather stupidly got off the omnibus just as it was flying at about ten thousand feet! With a cry of "I see London!" (followed by one of "Owch!") he plunged to earth. His badly bashed body was later found near Bermondsey gas works!

The London ghost bus

There's plenty of room on top and loads more downstairs. In fact this red double decker is completely empty. But if you see it ... ignore it! Because it's not got a driver or conductor. It's got a number seven on the front and people say they've seen it tearing around Kensington all on its own, frightening upper-class motorists out of their luxury car-coats. It usually goes on the rampage when all normal self-respecting buses are safely tucked up in their garages.

The Archduke Franz's banger

It wasn't really a banger, it was actually a mega-posh, red, open-topped limo that Archduke Franz Ferdinand had bought to impress the neighbours, like Germany and Bulgaria, not to mention the whole population of the Austrian Empire, which he just happened to be heir to! Anyway, he was out cruising in it one day in 1914, drawing admiring glances from the crowds when up popped a revolutionary who shot him and his duchess dead. And that sparked off the First World War with its casualty list of 20 million dead!

After the war the governor of Yugoslavia bought the car and fixed it up a bit but he still managed to have four accidents in it, including the one in which he lost his right arm. So he said it was definitely jinxed and should be trashed, but his pal Dr Srikis thought otherwise and had several months of carefree motoring in it – until the day it flipped over and squashed him dead.

The next owner was also a doctor but when his superstitious patients got wind of his spooky new wheels they deserted him in droves so he sold it to a Swiss racing driver who managed to prang it in a race and fatally break his neck. The car conked out for its next owner, a farmer, so he got his pal to give him a tow. Mid-tow, the cursed car roared into life, sent the tow car flying and killed both of them!

The last owner of the car said something like, "Oh, all it needs is a nice new colour and zen ze curse will be gone!" So he had it repainted a nice cheerful blue and drove himself and four pals to a wedding party in it. All five of them were killed in a head-on crash before they even reached the knees up!

The car was finally put in a museum in Vienna where its attendant Karl was fond of saying to people, "It is cursed. You must not sit in it. As long as you don't, everything will be fine!" And then World War Two started and some rotter dropped several hundred tons of high explosive on the museum, and Karl, *and* the car, blowing all three of them to smithereens. Cars ... who'd have 'em!

The phantom bi-plane of Weybridge

When there's a thunderstorm over Weybridge in Surrey, England two things usually happen. One: it rains a lot.

Two: people hear the sound of one of those old-fashioned "wing-sandwich" biplanes. They reckon it's being flown by a pilot who was killed during a thunderstorm in 1935.

Odd one out: "The Celestial Omnibus", is a short story by E M Forster (1879–1970). But all the rest are ... TRUE! (Well, sort of.)

Epilogue

Are you any the wiser then? Do they exist, or don't they? Maybe after reading that lot you've no doubts whatsoever that ghosts *do* exist and you're now scared stiff of your own shadow and your neck aches from constantly looking over your shoulder.

Or maybe you're so completely convinced that there's no such thing as ghosts that you'd spend a night in the most haunted house in the world with not so much as a mobile phone for company. No matter what *you* think, you can be sure that lots of other people will carry on believing in ghosts, and "seeing" them, *and* making up great stories about them. It's happening all the time.

Perhaps all these ghost stories have inspired you to write at least one of your own? One of the most popular sorts of modern ghost stories are "phantom hitch-hiker" stories. They're what are known as modern urban myths – in other words, they're invented stories about modern life that are passed on as if they are actually true. There are hundreds, maybe even thousands, of them. They're repeatedly told and retold, and as they are, little sections get chopped and changed. However, they more or less have the same basic ingredients and structure. So what better way to get started than to have a bash at your very own phantom hitch-hiker tale!

Here's a DIY multiple-choice one to get you going. Just copy or read out the story, selecting whichever multiple-choice word or phrase you fancy. But watch out, you might scare yourself, er ... silly?

The classic phantom hitch-hiker story – DIY version

Late one night a man was driving his *car / carpet / kangaroo / flock of sheep* down a lonely country *drainpipe / lane / stream /cliff face* in *Brazil / Dagenham / Devon / his pyjamas*. Suddenly his headlights picked out the figure of a *stunningly beautiful / hideously greasy / completely gormless / totally hairy ... princess / girl / TV soap starlet* standing by the side of the road. She appeared to be in *distress / dat dress / dem trainers / dese carpet slippers* and was frantically *waving her legs in the air / picking her nose / thumbing a lift / scratching her bottom*.

The man quickly drew *to a halt / a picture of a pony / five thousand pounds from his piggy bank* and offered her a *packet of prawn crackers / lift / escalator*. She immediately got *him in a headlock / in the car / her sixty mates out of the bushes* then sat *shivering / gibbering / steaming* on his *dashboard / back seat / knee*. The man asked her where *elephants go when they die / he could*

buy some really juicy satsumas / she wanted to be dropped off and she gave him a *swift smack in the chops/ an address in a nearby town / a really interesting talk on old mine shafts.* Noticing that she was *cold and wet / unbelievably dim / melting rapidly / swelling to the size of a hot air balloon* the man took pity on her and lent her his *coat / chest wig / pet chihuahua* so she could wrap it around her *shoulders / tongue / tonsils* and keep warm.

As they neared the local town he turned to speak to the girl but was horrified to see that she had *vanished / exploded / turned into a sausage.* However, in the exact spot where she'd been sitting the seat was *covered in dandruff / sopping wet / really badly scorched.* He stopped at a house in the town and knocked on the door. An old man and woman answered it and when the man described his mysterious passenger to them they told him that she was their *pet budgie / daughter / postman* who'd been *flogged off cheap at at car boot sale / given a part in an urban myth / killed in a road accident ... exactly twenty years ago / sometime during the last Ice Age / the previous Tuesday.* When they showed him the girl's *spare wooden teeth / photo / fingerprint / teddy* he recognized her immediately! They said she was buried at the local *graveyard / rubbish tip / fruit and veg market* so he went there straight away and found her *gravestone / gravy boat / grape stone*. Draped over it was his very own *overcoat / chest wig / pet chihuahua!*

Ooower! / So what? / Gerrawaywivyer!

THE END